DESERT SHOWDOWN

"Look out!" yelled a voice.

Noel spun around in the direction of the galloping hoofbeats coming his way. The flames roared to the sky, lighting up the world. The rider approaching him was hatless, and for a split second Noel saw his face clearly.

He saw the lean face that was so similar to his own. The dark brows, the gray eyes, the mouth set into a grim line . . . Noel felt the shock of recognition and a growing dismay.

"Leon!" he shouted.

His duplicate did not slow down the big horse. A girl in a long, pale dress lay limp across the front of his saddle. Leon raised a pistol and aimed it at Noel.

Without conscious thought Noel raised his own weapon and squeezed the trigger.

It clicked on an empty chamber. . . .

Ace Books by Sean Dalton

TIME⚬TRAP
SHOWDOWN

Operation StarHawks Series

SPACE HAWKS
CODE NAME PEREGRINE
BEYOND THE VOID
THE ROSTMA LURE
DESTINATION: MUTINY
THE SALUKAN GAMBIT

SHOWDOWN

SEAN DALTON

ACE BOOKS, NEW YORK

This book is an Ace original edition, and has never
been previously published.

SHOWDOWN

An Ace Book / published by arrangement with
the author

PRINTING HISTORY
Ace edition / July 1992

All rights reserved.
Copyright © 1992 by Deborah Chester.
Cover art by Dorian Vallejo.
This book may not be reproduced in whole or
in part, by mimeograph or any other means, without
permission. For information address:
The Berkley Publishing Group,
200 Madison Avenue, New York, New York 10016.

ISBN: 0-441-81257-0

Ace Books are published by The Berkley Publishing Group,
200 Madison Avenue, New York, New York 10016.
The name "ACE" and the "A" logo are trademarks
belonging to Charter Communications, Inc.

PRINTED IN THE UNITED STATES OF AMERICA

10 9 8 7 6 5 4 3 2 1

This book is dedicated with respect and love to my grandfather, Lewis Dalton Hatcher, who gave me childhood summers of cowpunching, fence building, water trough cleaning, and branding under the wide New Mexico sky. No kid could have had it any better.

PaPa, here's the western you asked for.

CHAPTER 1

Drowning was no fun.

Materializing on the other side of the time vortex, historian Noel Kedran expected to find himself safely home in the familiar twenty-sixth-century surroundings of the Time Institute.

Instead, he was caught unexpectedly in a swift current of water, suddenly struggling for his life, with no time to wonder where he was or how he came to be in this rushing, roiling torrent. Water roared around him, foaming creamy slobbers and sloshing sometimes higher than his bobbing head.

He flailed out in confusion, his survival instinct forcing him to swim even before his mind could comprehend what had happened. It was hard to see, hard to keep his head above water. The sunlight overhead was blinding. The water was opaque with mud and debris. It stank.

He tried to stroke against the current, but it was too powerful. A tangled mess of tree limbs swept over him without warning, pushing him beneath the surface to be tumbled and battered among the rocks. Desperately he clawed his way back to the surface, broke through, and dragged in a mighty breath. His arms and legs felt leaden. His medieval clothes—especially the knee-length tunic—weighed him down. He felt the temptation to let the current sweep him wherever it wanted. But if this was a river, he knew he could not last in the water indefinitely. He started swimming toward the bank again.

Constantly swirled around and tumbled, he caught only glimpses of the banks rushing by. They were steep rock faces on both sides, narrow like a canyon. They were too sheer to climb, even if he reached them, but he hoped to catch hold of *something* before he was pounded to death between the water and the rocks.

Some object struck his shoulder, spinning him around. He fought to keep his head aloft, and one of his flailing hands touched wet hair. The object was a dead antelope, tan and cream, with staring chocolate eyes. Before he could react, another tangle of tree limbs overtook him and drove him deep beneath the surface.

He hit his head, and a white explosion went off inside his skull. His limbs went slack, and by sheer willpower alone he clung to consciousness, holding on against the dark death that awaited him. The spin of the water bobbed him back to the surface. Desperately he dragged in a breath. Water slopped into his mouth. He choked and went under again.

For an instant it seemed almost too difficult to go on fighting. But Noel wasn't a quitter. With the last reserves of his strength, he made the surface again, aware that his odds of survival were worsening. What was that old principle of drowning? The third time you went down, you stayed down? He'd gone under twice.

But then the steep canyon walls dropped to low dirt banks, and the water spread out into a sandy draw that absorbed and slowed its brutal progress.

SHOWDOWN

When the force of the current slackened, Noel kicked out with renewed hope, angling toward the bank. This time he made headway. A tumbleweed floated by, just inches from his face. He found himself staring into the yellow eyes of a snake wound up inside the tumbleweed.

His stroke faltered, and something bulky rammed him from behind. Noel whirled around, every nerve screaming, and saw it was a man, floating limp in the water.

Unconscious or dead, Noel couldn't tell. He snagged the man's arm, then grabbed him around the middle, momentarily giving up his chance of reaching the bank. Instead, he grabbed a passing fence post and clung to it with wet-slick fingers, keeping the man's head out of the water.

In a few minutes the draw's sandy banks dropped still lower to almost nothing. The water petered away into dozens of tiny side draws, and its force abated. Noel's knees dragged the bottom. He released the post, letting it float on, and half dragged, half floated the man to the bank.

Noel heaved him onto shore first, then climbed out beside him and collapsed, winded and so tired he could hardly see. He knew he should check his companion in case resuscitation procedures were called for, but he needed to catch his own breath first. He closed his eyes to fight off dizziness.

When he reopened them an unknown amount of time later, he was conscious of overwhelming heat. Sunlight burned through his lashes when he squinted open his eyes. It was harsh light—dazzling, merciless. He felt like he'd been baked.

Slowly, aching all over, he sat up and looked around. The water had receded from his feet. Small puddles dotted the bottom of the draw. Most of them were already forming a scum and drying up. At his movement, birds and lizards scuttled away from the small water holes. Across the draw, he saw a flash of tawny fur bound through the brush and vanish before he could determine what it was.

It was wide, empty country—as stark and bleak as anything he could imagine. A cloudless sky of cobalt-blue stretched forever. The tawny ground supported only scrub and weeds. Out beyond the draw ran a low strip of flat ground about fifty meters wide. It was filled with clumps of dead grass that grew in knee-high, skeletal tufts. Here and there, a variety of cactus bristled tall, snakelike arms to the sky, its pink blooms vivid against such desiccated surroundings.

Noel rubbed his face, trying to piece together what had happened. He was a historian, a time traveler. He'd been on his way home from medieval Greece, but instead of landing back in bustling, overcrowded Chicago at the Time Institute, he was here in this desert wasteland.

A shadow flitted over him. Startled, he glanced up and saw buzzards wheeling in the sky. He got to his feet and waved at them, but they didn't leave.

His companion moaned.

Noel knelt beside him and rolled him over onto his back. He was a boy, not a man—perhaps sixteen or seventeen years old—but already honed to sinewy steel by this harsh country. His tanned jaw showed the faint blond beginnings of a beard, and his hair was a light, streaky brown beneath its crust of dried sand. He wore a shirt of rough cotton, a faded red bandanna twisted about his throat, long trousers with an empty gun holster, and high-heeled boots of scuffed cowhide.

Noel frowned, not wanting to believe that he was in the old West. He checked the boy's pulse and found it steady. A darkening bruise on the boy's temple seemed to be his only injury. He would be coming awake soon.

After a split second of hesitation, Noel made a swift search of the boy's pockets. He found a U.S. silver dollar stamped 1885, a cloth bag of waterlogged tobacco, a sheaf of ruined cigarette papers, and a dog-eared sepia photograph of an unsmiling girl in a white dress embellished with lace and ribbons. Her hair was pulled back with a broad ribbon. She looked enough like the boy to be his sister. Frowning, Noel turned the coin over in his fingers several times. It was worn rather than new-minted, but it gave him the information he needed. He placed the items back in the boy's pockets.

It was likely he'd saved this boy's life. And if that meant another change of history that he was going to have to correct, he did not want to deal with it now. He had enough complications on his hands, just being here.

Besides, it was time to find out where here was.

Noel looked around and headed for the cover of a massive, squat mesquite bush growing over a mound of earth riddled with holes. Noel guessed it was a rat den. At any rate he hoped it was a den for rats rather than snakes. He crouched cautiously near the bush and started the routine self-check that was mandatory for any Traveler.

He still wore his medieval garb of long tunic and hose, and already he was roasting in the light wool cloth. His blue hose were ripped and encrusted with sand and dried mud. He shucked them off, then put back on his cloth shoes with their thin leather soles. His legs were pale in the harsh sunlight. Pretty soon they would be lobster red. He didn't think his footgear would be of much use in this country of scorpions and rattlesnakes, but the shoes were all he had. Ripping the long sleeves off his tunic, he discovered the arrow wound in his shoulder was gone.

Noel flexed his left arm experimentally. It was as good as ever, although his muscles were still tired from the swim. That was one of the better side effects of time travel. It accelerated healing at an unheard-of rate, as though growth cells were stimulated. Yet the side effects did not include corresponding aging.

A lizard flicked by, and Noel flinched. An image of the diamondback rattler wound in that floating tumbleweed returned to him, as vivid as life, and still scary. He listened to a gentle but steady breeze rustle through the clusters of drying mesquite beans hanging from the thorny branches of the bush and imagined he could hear snake rattles.

This country was stark, primitive, savage. He tried to tell himself that he was still jumpy from materializing in the wrong place, but deep down he knew better. He had the sense of being watched, although the only living things he could see around him were a pair of jackrabbits, the lizards, and the buzzards still wheeling patiently overhead. Only the toughest could survive in this land. The heat was intense, smothering him, baking harshly into his brain. He squinted at the sun, and judged it nearly noon. He needed to find shelter.

He was acutely conscious of thirst. His mouth felt as though it had been scoured with sand. He could barely work up enough spit to swallow. And of course, he felt the pangs of intense hunger that traveling always brought on.

At least, however, he still had his LOC. The Light Operated Computer was programmed with molecular shift capability and could disguise itself to blend in with destination and time. Noel examined a wide cuff of Indian silver on his left wrist. Turquoise studded the metal in a handsome design. But this was not the time to admire it.

"LOC, activate," he said in a low, urgent voice.

The computer hummed softly to life, shimmering into its true configuration of a clear-sided bracelet that pulsed with a complexity of miniature fiber-optic circuits.

"Working," it said.

"No, you're not," snapped Noel, shoving his fingers through his black hair. "What the hell are we doing here? We're supposed to be home in Chicago. Twenty-sixth century, remember? Can't you get anything right?"

The computer made no reply. With a sigh, Noel realized he'd asked it too many questions at once. He hauled his temper under control.

"Okay, let's start again. Specify time and location."

"New Mexico territory, year 1887."

Noel's puzzlement grew. It made no sense for him to be here. A trained historian and experienced time traveler, his speciality was classical antiquity—the Greek, Roman, and Egyptian variety. His mission was to visit events of historical significance and make recordings of what transpired. With his own century marred by social unrest, a widening gap between uneducated labor and technocrats, and the population's increasing dependence on fantasy, drugs, and head chips, Noel sought to bring back evidence of courage, involvement, and valor. Civilization in the twenty-sixth century had stretched about as far as it could go. It was teetering on the edge. Anarchists were doing their best to bring everything down. Noel felt a commitment to saving mankind by showing it examples from the best moments of the past.

However, on his last mission anarchist saboteurs had tampered with his LOC, and he had found himself in the wrong place and time. But he'd been certain he'd corrected his LOC. Apparently, he was wrong.

What was special about New Mexico in the late 1800's? He couldn't think of anything. It was a time of settlement and expansion. The worst of the Indian uprisings had been suppressed. The massive cattle drives along the Chisum trail were probably being replaced by railroads shipping steers to market. So why was he here?

He recalled that medieval Greece was a rather obscure part of history as well. Perhaps his LOC had somehow been reprogrammed to send him *away* from anywhere significant.

The awful dread that he was never going to get back to his own time grew in Noel. "Why are we here?" he asked the LOC.

"Unknown."

"Dammit!"

The LOC waited, humming to itself.

Noel started to count to ten but gave up at three. "We were on set recall coordinates, correct?"

"Acknowledged."

"Recall failed. Why?"

The LOC hummed for a few seconds. Noel forced himself to wait despite the impatient urge to pound the device with the nearest rock. Those saboteurs back home had really messed it up. He was supposed to get lightning answers to his questions. He was supposed to have full information access from extensive data banks. He was supposed to come and go on the correct time stream and materialize where he belonged, not be jerked randomly through time and space.

"LOC!" he snapped. "Respond. Why did recall fail?"

"Working," said the LOC almost sullenly. "Recall did not fail."

He could have yelled. He could have pulled off the LOC and thrown it into the farthest mesquite bush. Neither alternative would help.

"What," he said sarcastically, "do you call where we are?"

"New Mexico territory, year 1887."

"I *know* that, you piece of junk. Recall was set for Chicago, year—"

"Recall limit reached," said the LOC flatly.

Noel's brows knotted, and he chewed on that unwelcome response for a while. Finally, in a quiet, almost hopeless voice he asked, "Is the time loop closed?"

"Affirmative."

"And its maximum limit points are 1332 and 1887?"

"Checking . . . affirmative."

Noel drew his knees up and rested his chin on them. He felt as though the bottom had dropped from his stomach. He felt cold and disassociated, as though pieces of himself had detached and were floating.

"Oh, God," he said softly, aware that he was truly and for all eternity trapped. Unless he could find a way for the LOC to repair itself, he would never see his own time again.

He had faced that possibility when he'd landed in medieval Greece by mistake. But he had managed to get the LOC to perform certain self-diagnostic and repair functions. He had corrected the anomalies caused by his presence in that time. He had thought everything was set up for his return home.

False hope.

A quavery whistle brought him from his reverie with a jerk.

"Roan?" called the boy. "Ro-an! Here, boy!"

Noel whispered, "Disguise mode."

The LOC blinked off and resumed its shape as the silver cuff. Noel climbed cautiously to his feet and went back to the draw. He kept to cover, not yet wanting to make his presence known, and watched the boy a moment. The boy was limping along the bank, scanning the plain anxiously. He whistled again, but without much conviction. Whoever he was looking for wasn't around.

Noel stepped into plain view, and said, "Hello."

The boy spun around fast, and reached for the gun that was missing from his holster. His eyes were blue and as big as saucers. It took him a second to realize his pistol was gone. He straightened, looking faintly sick. Noel saw him swallow.

"Easy," said Noel in a quiet, steady voice. "I'm a friend."

He stepped forward, but the boy stumbled back. Noel stopped, afraid the boy was going to back himself right off the bank of the draw.

"Friend," said Noel.

The boy swallowed again, then steeled himself. "No 'pache is my friend."

He spoke English in the broken, gruff-shrill range of a boy-man. A tide of red flooded his cheeks, but his eyes held steady with Noel's.

Noel smiled. "You mean Apache? As in Indian? Son, I'm neither."

"Oh." The boy blinked, then pointed at Noel's clothing. "You're rigged out like one. You live with them maybe?"

"No. It's either wear this or go buck naked." Noel grinned. "There are a few places where I'd just as soon not be sunburned."

The boy grinned back, then ducked his head. "My mistake, I guess. No offense?"

"None taken. I'm Noel Kedran."

Noel held out his hand, and after a moment of hesitation the boy came forward and shook. His hand was strong and work-callused.

"Cody Trask. I'm with the Double T outfit. I sure thought I was a goner when I got caught in that flash flood. Did you pull me out?"

Noel nodded, then glanced at the sky in puzzlement. It was cloudless. "I didn't know a storm could come and go so fast."

The boy laughed in astonishment. "Mister, there ain't been no storm here. Couple of nights ago it rained hard up in those mountains yonder." He pointed north, and Noel saw a dim purple smudge of a mountain range on the far horizon. "Reckon this water came down from them."

It was Noel's turn to be astonished. "Impossible. Water wouldn't run that far. Those mountains are miles away."

"Yep. That's the way it happens in this country. You think this draw was made by 'paches using shovels?"

Noel realized the boy was no longer looking at him with wariness. Instead, amusement gleamed in those large blue eyes along with some good-natured scorn.

Before Noel could answer, the boy pointed southeast at the tufts of dead grass. "Look at all this good tobosa grass. It's here because water comes here. The better the grass, the more water has been coming down this draw."

Noel wondered about the blow the boy had taken on the head. Gently he said, "The grass is dead."

"Naw! It's greening up some. We had a trace of rain a week or so back. Now this flood will bring it out quick. I'll have to tell Uncle Frank to push the springin' heifers this way." He paused and worry returned to his face. "That is, if I can find Roan."

"Who's Roan?"

"My horse. Best one I ever had too. You seen him?"

Noel shook his head. He thought about miles of desolate country, fierce heat, and no transportation. "How far are we from where you live?"

Cody squinted into the distance and nibbled on the corner of his mouth. "Now that's a good question. I went into the draw probably about a mile or so up. That stupid maverick kept trying to run off from me. Didn't want to be driven anywhere. Otherwise I wouldn't have ridden the draw. Uncle Frank will call me a chucklehead for sure. And if I've lost Roan—"

"How far?"

"Oh, I reckon we're about fifteen miles from the headquarters. Up over those little ridges yonder is a line cabin about five or six miles. But I don't think we ought to go that way. Skeet said last night he'd heard some Comancheros had started raiding up from the border."

"The Mexican border?" asked Noel.

"Sure." Cody frowned. "You ain't from around here, are you, mister?"

"Call me Noel. No, I'm not. I'm from . . . Chicago."

Cody blinked, looking impressed. "Golly! That's back East somewhere."

"North."

"Big city?"

Noel squinted. "Very."

"I thought you talked like a tenderfoot. No offense."

Noel smiled. "That's me." He pointed at his cloth shoes. "Especially if we have to walk fifteen miles in these."

"I never seen moccasins like those before. Uncle Frank says it ain't polite to ask folks about themselves, but you been with the 'paches, or something?"

It was the easiest explanation. "Yes," said Noel.

"Golly! They've had you for a slave, haven't they? Dressed you like a squaw and all. No offense. Did they torture you?"

"No."

"Whose band was it?"

"I don't know."

"How long were you a prisoner? Where did they capture you? Did they get any of your friends? How did you get away?"

"I jumped in the water," said Noel. "Now enough questions. We can't stand around in this heat all day. I feel like my brain is melting."

Cody bent over and brushed the sand from his hair. "I reckon I lost my hat. Let's go up the bank a ways and look for Roan."

"The horse would have come by now if he heard you calling."

"Maybe. And maybe he's already lit out for home. Uncle Frank is going to tan my hide for this. That maverick steer probably drowned his stupid self, and now I'll be coming in afoot."

"You'll get your horse back, I'm sure," said Noel.

"Naw, it ain't a ten-dollar horse Uncle Frank'll be mad about. It's my saddle and my rope. Both new." Cody turned red. "I just had me a birthday about a week back."

"Congratulations. Let's—"

Cody glanced past Noel's shoulder and without warning he went tense and still. Then he grabbed Noel's arm in a grip like steel and pulled him down behind a bush.

Noel slithered around in the hot sand on his knees and looked where Cody was staring. He saw the series of small, stony ridges to the south, a few tall yucca plants in white bloom, and cactus. Nothing else. A hawk sailed across the sky, and the earth was hot, empty, and silent.

"What—"

"Quiet!" whispered Cody. His eyes were round and tense. Noel could see the pulse hammering in his temple. "I saw a mirror flash. If another answers..."

He didn't finish his sentence.

Noel wondered why in the world they should worry about a mirror flash, but he kept quiet and thought it out. Steel mirrors were used for hand signals, swift communication in a land devoid of electronics.

"Who?" he whispered.

"It could be a couple of 'paches signaling each other," muttered Cody. "Or maybe I just saw the sun flash off a silver concha on somebody's saddle. I don't see nothin' now. You?"

"No."

Noel was having trouble adjusting to long-distance visibility. The idea of seeing someone a mile or more away made him feel twice as exposed and vulnerable as before. He stared at the ridges until his eyes burned, but he saw no riders.

"Yep, I see 'em," said Cody grimly. He pointed. "Just for a moment they went over the top of the ridge and were above the skyline. Maybe a half dozen. Must be Comancheros. 'Paches don't like to ride horses much."

"What are Comancheros?" asked Noel.

Cody shot him a serious, worried look. "Nobody you want to tangle with if you can help it. I reckon we'd better hightail it out of here."

CHAPTER 2

They made poor time at first, for Cody insisted on keeping to cover and every half hour or so he crouched down and watched their back trail for a while to make certain they weren't being followed.

Parched, parboiled, and drenched with sweat, Noel got tired of all the caution and said so. "Looks to me like we're clear."

Cody grunted. "Uncle Frank says that when everything looks most peaceful and safe, that's when you ought to keep one hand on your gun and the other on your scalp."

With his knife, Cody cut off the top of a barrel cactus and dug out some of the soft, moist insides. Noel sniffed the stuff with reluctance, but when Cody put it in his mouth and chewed on it, Noel did the same. The little taste it had was bitter. It didn't contain enough moisture to make a difference. After a few moments, Noel spat it out. Cody did the same and wiped his chapped lips.

"Sure do miss my hat," he said, glancing up at the merciless sun. "Least it ain't July. We'd be fair cooked by now."

Noel felt cooked enough. They were heading west, and the

steady breeze from that direction increased as the afternoon wore on. It was a desert wind, dry and lacking even a trace of coolness. Noel's arms and legs were sunburned. His face hurt from sun and wind. He quit talking. He quit watching the country around them. He just concentrated on putting his feet in the boy's tireless tracks.

By the time the sun was slipping low ahead of them, the flat mesquite country had changed. Reddish, sandy earth had become powdery chalk that floated up from their dragging feet to coat their clothing and choke their nostrils. The ground grew rocky and sported a thin silky grass with tufts. Little dips and ridges made the going slower.

Noel had worn through his thin soles. He was limping on some thorns he'd picked up. Cody looked drawn and gray-faced. One of his boot soles came loose, and he tied it back together with his belt. A roadrunner trotted ahead of them for a few yards, then flicked its long tail and veered into the greasewood. Grasshoppers jumped in waves away from them. Cactus wrens fluttered and chirped busily in the brush.

Noel and Cody crested a ridge overlooking a narrow arroyo choked with brush and tumbled boulders. There they took a rest, making sure they were below the skyline. Noel groaned as he sat down. He wasn't sure he would be able to get up and walk again. Right now, the way his muscles were protesting, he could lie here on the stones and the cactus and sleep forever.

"We're almost home," said Cody. He slapped some of the dust off his trousers. "This here is the horse pasture. Just a quarter section in these little valleys and all, but there's good grama grass for them to eat."

Noel rubbed his face. He had no interest in grass. His own stomach felt so hollow he thought his ribs might collapse. A jackrabbit crouched about twenty feet away, long ears shining pink in the approaching sunset. He thought about the taste of rabbit meat and licked his lips.

"How close is almost home?" he asked.

" 'Bout a half mile. Maybe less. I sure hope José has already started cooking on that big feast he's planning for tonight. I could eat a whole bull calf all by myself. Uncle Frank and Grandpa rode off to town yesterday to meet the stage. They're supposed to bring my sister Lisa-Marie home tonight."

Shyly Cody pulled out the photograph of the girl Noel had examined earlier. Noel pretended to look at it closely.

"She resembles you."

"Yeah, we're twins. I ain't seen her in five years though. Uncle Frank packed her off to boarding school in Santa Fe when my ma died. He said the ranch wasn't no place for a girl. I reckon that's so, but she'll be a stranger to me now."

"Maybe not."

Cody snorted. "Well, look at her. Wearing a fancy dress and all la-di-dah with ribbons in her hair. The last time I saw her she was wearing some of my pants and 'pache moccasins, her hair in pigtails, and screaming Mexican cuss words at the top of her lungs while Uncle Frank drove her off to town in the buckboard."

Noel had to laugh. "I take it she didn't want to go."

"Naw. I figured she'd run away and be back down here in a few weeks, but she didn't. She stayed the whole time until she graduated. Now she's all educated and different, and what Uncle Frank thinks he's going to do with her is—"

He broke off, turning his head, and sniffed. "You smell that?"

Noel put his nostrils in the breeze, which had grown still when the sun started to go down, but had now picked up again. The wind was cool on his bare arms, raising goose bumps through his sunburn.

"Smoke?" he said at last.

Cody climbed to his feet. "Shouldn't be any. I haven't seen signs of a fire."

The boy looked worried again. Without a word, Noel pushed himself to his feet, biting back a moan, and forced his stiffening muscles to move. The boy was already striding out, setting a fast pace that soon left Noel lagging behind.

In the slow-gathering twilight, the rocky shale made footing treacherous. Noel slithered and stubbed his toes. He kept a wary eye out for snakes, but Cody was nearly running now with all caution forgotten. The smell of smoke grew steadily stronger. It wasn't the light, savory-scented smoke of a campfire made from sagebrush or greasewood. No, it was heavy, acrid . . . the smell of a serious fire.

Ahead, a fat column of black rose into the purple sky, its menace silhouetted against the coral sunset.

"The ranch!" choked Cody. "Somebody's burning the ranch! Oh, God, I got to stop them! I got to—"

"Hold it!" shouted Noel, lunging to grab his arm and sling him around. Cody struggled, swinging a wild fist that Noel ducked. He caught the boy by both arms and shook him. "You can't just go charging in. You lost your gun, remember? What are you going to do?"

Cody's eyes looked black in the shadows. He wrenched free. "I got to stop it."

He plunged on, and Noel ran after him.

They heaved and clawed their way up a gulch that sliced a steep slope. Cody never hesitated at the top, but Noel took the crest cautiously and paused there to take in the sight.

The ranch headquarters stood cupped in a protected area, bounded on three sides by ridges, with a sloping vista spreading out from it to the south. A pair of mighty cottonwoods shaded a small dirt tank built to hold the runoff water pumped by the windmill. The barn and corrals stood some distance away from the other buildings. Livestock milled uneasily within the pens. The main house was a large rambling affair of adobe, fitted with a tiled roof. There couldn't be much of it that would burn, unless there were ceiling timbers, but tall flames were raging through the shattered windows, seeking air, and the less substantial bunkhouse was entirely engulfed, its wooden frame barely seen through the yellow-white fire.

Men on horseback were circling at a safe distance from the fire. Noel could hear them shouting, and some fired their pistols into the air. A girl's scream pierced the noise.

"Lisa-Marie!" shouted Cody.

"Cody, no!"

But Cody didn't hear. He ran at the horsemen, yelling like a madman. One of the desperadoes saw him coming and laughed.

"Hey, amigos! It is another one, eh? *Olé!*"

He spurred his horse at Cody, and the animal's shoulder knocked Cody spinning. The boy staggered and fell to one knee. The horseman wheeled his mount and came at him again just as Cody struggled back to his feet. The man struck Cody across the face with his big sombrero. Cody, however, seized his wrist, and nearly dragged the man from the saddle.

The man wrenched free, and swung his pistol viciously. Even from a distance, Noel heard the thud of it hitting Cody in the face. Cody crumpled in a heap, and Noel's temper snapped.

There wasn't much cover, but the men's attention was still on the fire and their own celebrations. Noel saw one rider pass a bottle to another. He crouched low and ran for the corrals, taking a risk on being seen, his heart whamming his rib cage like thunder.

He made it without being spotted, and clung a moment to the board fence. What he needed was a diversion and a weapon. The girl's scream came again, a sobbing desperate cry that made the hair on the back of his neck stand up. He gritted his teeth and forced himself into action.

Over to one side of the corrals stood a buckboard wagon with a dome-lid trunk and some carpetbags still strapped to the back. The horses had been unharnessed, but among the milling animals inside the corral, he saw one with a saddle on.

Noel slipped into the midst of the frightened horses. They were rumbling and snorting, shaking their heads, their ears working in alarm. The fire threw eerie shadows across their backs. Noel spoke softly to them as he worked his way through their midst. It seemed to take an eternity to get to the saddled horse. At last, however, he grabbed the one he wanted. It shied, but he grasped the bridle and hung on grimly, making soothing sounds to it and stroking its neck until it quieted.

Untying the reins from where they'd been looped around the saddle horn, he felt for a saddle holster and found none. Well, a six-shooter would have been too much luck to hope for. He noticed one of the top boards of the fence had warped in the sun and weather. One end had come loose from a post, and the nails showed. He grasped it, getting a palm full of splinters, and managed to pull the whole board loose.

A piece of wood wasn't much against men with pistols, but he didn't much care for types who attacked houses about suppertime, set fire to them, beat up young boys, and made pretty girls scream. Swinging into the saddle, he balanced the board across the saddle horn, then bent over and unlatched the gate.

The horses milled and shied back. Then one saw freedom and lunged for it. The others followed, galloping full-tilt.

Noel held his quivering mount on a tight rein until all the others were out, then he gave slack. His horse nearly bolted out from under him, snorting and fighting the bit. He crouched low, clutching his board, and stayed at the rear of the herd until they swept past the burning house and veered from it.

Noel tugged hard on the reins and forced his bucking, protesting mount straight at the nearest desperado. The man saw him and yelled a warning that was cut short with a mighty oomph when Noel whacked him across the middle with the board.

Mexican curses filled the air. A shot whizzed over Noel's head. He ducked, and again his nervous mount nearly shied out from under him. Fighting to regain control of his horse, Noel wrenched the animal around and went galloping straight at the next man, yelling at the top of his lungs and swinging the board like a club.

The man shot at him, but the bullet went wide. Noel was too crazy to care. He hit the man with a mighty crunch. Screaming, the Mexican tumbled off the back of his horse.

Something plucked at the shoulder of Noel's tunic. He heard a flat-crack sound, and an angry hum like a hornet. The bullets were getting closer. He had two down, and how many to go?

A rifle opened fire—its sound heavy and vicious above the pistols. Noel's momentary craziness faded to fear, until he saw one of the desperadoes go tumbling and realized he had an ally.

Noel tossed aside his board and jumped off his horse, letting it shy free of him and run, reins dangling. He ran to the fallen man and scooped up his pistol.

It was a heavy Colt .45, long-barreled and awkward. He hoped it had some bullets left in it.

Before he could check, a hoarse yell made him look up in time to see a rider bearing down on him at a gallop. From that angle it looked like the orange flames shooting everywhere had formed a halo around this man. Noel glimpsed a flash of white teeth in the shadows beneath the wide hat brim and guessed the man was either saying his prayers or cursing Noel to perdition.

Noel had no time to aim. He shot the man's horse in the neck. Horse and rider went down almost on top of Noel. He sidestepped and saw the rider kick free of the stirrups even as the horse was falling in a headlong tumble. Noel launched himself in a furious tackle, bringing down the rider before he could scramble clear.

The man stank of whiskey and sweat. His leather jacket was greasy with age and kept Noel from getting a good hold on him. He fought mean and dirty, kicking and gouging, but Noel managed to hit him in the head with his pistol, and the man went slack beneath him.

Gasping, Noel straightened and wiped the sweat from his face with an unsteady hand. After the rough, intense action, he felt disoriented for a moment and had to look around to regain his bearings.

"Look out!" yelled a voice.

Noel spun around in the direction of galloping hoofbeats coming his way. The flames roared to the sky, lighting up the world. The rider approaching him was hatless, and for a split second Noel saw his face clearly.

He saw the lean face that was so similar to his own. The dark brows, the gray eyes, the mouth set in a grim line . . . Noel felt the shock of recognition and a growing dismay.

"Leon!" he shouted.

His duplicate had first been created in the anomaly caused by a malfunctioning time stream. Noel had hoped that when he left medieval Greece, he left Leon as well, but it seemed his twin had followed him here to this time and place.

"Leon!" he shouted again.

His duplicate did not slow the big horse. A girl in a long,

pale dress lay limp across the front of his saddle. Leon raised a pistol and aimed it at Noel.

Without conscious thought Noel raised his own weapon and squeezed the trigger.

It clicked on an empty chamber.

Defenseless, Noel's blood ran cold. Leon had tried to kill him before. Now he had the perfect chance.

Leon reined the horse to a halt, making it rear. He took deliberate, point-blank aim. His eyes were crazy with rage and hatred.

Noel couldn't speak. He couldn't move.

Then a rifle shot whined through the air, and Leon's pistol went flying. Leon jerked his hand and swore in pain.

"Adios, brother," he sneered, shaking the blood from his injured fingers onto Noel. "We shall meet again. Next time I won't miss."

Before Noel could respond, Leon wheeled his horse and lashed it on both shoulders with the long reins. The animal galloped into the darkness, and all was silent.

The fire inside the adobe house was starting to die down. With a sudden roar, the bunkhouse collapsed, sending sparks and cinders gusting skyward. Noel flinched, but he didn't see that even a bucket brigade between the dirt tank and the house could have any effect on the fire now.

He started to go check on Cody, but before he'd taken more than a couple of steps in that direction, a gruff voice said, "Hold it right there! Stand in your tracks, and put your hands up."

The voice, disembodied, might have come from anywhere. Noel suspected it was from somewhere behind him, close to the house. If it went with the finger that had been firing the rifle, he wasn't going to argue.

He stood still and put up his hands.

"Get rid of that hogleg."

Noel frowned. "What?"

"The pistol! Drop it!"

"It's empty."

"Mister," grated the voice in a tone that brooked no argument, "I ain't gonna waste my bullets kicking up dust around your feet. If I have to shoot to convince you to do what I say, I'm gonna put a bullet in your hide, where it'll do some good."

Noel dropped the pistol. His back itched, and he wondered exactly where the rifle sights were centered.

"That's better. Now you turn around nice and slow."

Noel complied.

"You catch the reins of that horse over there and you lead him this way."

Noel had trouble catching the animal, which was inclined to shy from him each time he reached for the dangling reins. Speaking soothingly to it, he finally grabbed the reins. He patted its neck and led it back toward the burning house.

"Stop there."

The old man came out of hiding, hobbling along on legs bent with rheumatism. He held a Winchester in his hands, and that long, deadly muzzle remained rock steady on Noel. The ruddy firelight gleamed off the man's thick white hair, showing a seamed, weathered face marked by a white mustache and fierce, jutting brows.

He glared at Noel, then watched his burning house for a moment, his throat working.

"Damned Comancheros," he muttered. "No call to burn an honest man out. I been here nigh on thirty years, trying to make a go of this place. Nana and Victorio went raiding through here, and they didn't burn me out. Ain't no one gonna burn me out."

He swung back to Noel.

SHOWDOWN

"Easy," said Noel swiftly, unsure of the old fellow's mood. "I'm a friend."

"The hell you say. All I see is a stranger without no pants on. Now you bring that horse over here to me, and you don't make no sudden moves."

"I don't think you should ride after Leon alone," said Noel in concern. "He's dangerous—"

"Shut up! You think I'm gonna sit here and hold my head while that varmint runs off with my granddaughter? I got to get her back."

"How are you going to chase them in the dark?" asked Noel.

"Son, the more you stand here jawin' the farther he's getting away." He jacked a fresh bullet into the chamber. "Now do what I say!"

There was no arguing with the rifle. Noel led the horse closer and held its bridle while the old man took the reins. They looked at each other, close up and eye to eye. Furious and raw with grief, the man was in no condition to be tracking anyone, least of all Leon. Noel knew this was his chance to jump him, rifle or no rifle.

He shifted his feet, and the old man flinched. The rifle roared at point-blank range, making the horse shy violently. Noel felt the bullet pluck his side, and adrenaline rushed to the top of his skull with such force it left him gasping and dizzy.

He stumbled back, scared and furious. "You crazy old fool!" he shouted. "I wasn't doing anything!"

The old man hauled himself, wheezing, into the saddle and wheeled the horse around. "The hell you weren't. I ought to put a bullet in you, same as your friends did to my family. My son and my grandson are both gone. But you ain't beat me yet. I swear to God and the devil both, I ain't beaten. Now, get out of my way."

He spurred the horse, and it leapt to a canter. Noel dodged to one side, and the big animal brushed past him. The shadows swallowed the old man, and a few minutes later the echo of hoofbeats faded away.

"Crazy old coot!" shouted Noel after him. His voice echoed back from the hills surrounding the ranch.

Swearing, Noel stuck his finger through the hole in the side of his tunic. It was a poor kind of gratitude he'd received for helping fight the outlaws. He hoped the old man's horse stepped in a rabbit hole and threw him out there in the dark.

No, he didn't.

Calming down a little, Noel wiped the soot and sweat from his face and figured that if he were in the old man's shoes he might well be acting the same way.

As for Leon being here . . . Noel frowned and swore again. He'd been convinced that Leon's existence was a fluke, a momentary glitch that would be erased through the recall process of the time stream.

Well, he'd been wrong. It looked like as long as Noel was trapped in this time loop, Leon was too.

And already Leon was causing trouble, meddling with people's lives, and doing his best to change history.

Noel sighed. He was going to have to help straighten this out. He was going to have to take care of his twin once and for all. Maybe that was the way to break free of this trap.

CHAPTER 3

Cody was lying facedown in the dirt when Noel found him. Gently Noel rolled him over and checked his pulse. It beat strong against his fingers. Relieved, Noel gave him a shake.

"Cody? Cody, wake up."

The boy didn't stir. This was twice in one day that he'd been hit in the head. Noel figured he'd be out cold for a long while.

Gathering the boy over his shoulder in a fireman's lift, Noel trudged back toward the barn. He'd already dragged the Comancheros into a tack room and dropped a bar across the door to lock them in. They were secured where they could cause no more trouble. Now all he had to do was get the boy bedded down in the barn, and find something to eat before he faded with hunger.

Soot and cinders were still raining down. A few sparks had caught in the broomweed growing in sparse clumps here and there. Tiny flames shot up swiftly, only to die almost at once as the weeds were consumed. The air stank of smoke.

Coughing, Noel settled the boy on a lumpy bed of feed sacks and covered him with an unfolded saddle blanket that smelled of dust and dried horse sweat. The night air was growing chilly. Noel shivered and went back outside to scavenge.

The boy had made references to his uncle Frank and a cook called José. Noel started looking for them. The cook he found dead in the rear courtyard of the house. The man had fallen beside the well, a rifle and his medallion of Mary clutched in his hands.

Noel closed the staring eyes, pocketed the medallion so it wouldn't get lost, and took possession of the rifle.

With the fire dying down, the night closed in. He heard coyotes howl in the distance. That primitive, eerie sound reached straight to Noel's primordial instincts. Shivers went up his spine. He gripped the rifle more tightly.

From the direction of the dirt tank an owl hooted softly from the cottonwood trees. Their leaves whispered in the night breeze. Beyond the barn and corrals, a pair of green eyes gleamed briefly in some trick of the firelight, then scuttled away.

Noel paused, the hair on the back of his neck prickling, his eyes scanning the darkness. Overhead, a multitude of stars—unscreened by smog, clouds, or the haze of city lights—filled the sky with abundance. Constellations stood out clearly. A shower of meteors zipped over the black horizon. One entered the atmosphere, and he saw the blaze of its trail for a few brief seconds before it passed from sight.

Something moaned.

He spun on his heel to crouch tensely, rifle aimed, ears straining. Seconds ticked by. His gaze scanned all directions, but he saw only shadows.

After a few moments his thudding heartbeat slowed down. He forced himself to draw in a deep breath. Time to take it easy. He'd had a hard day. Exhaustion was playing tricks on him.

The moan came again.

He thought it was in the direction of the corrals. Empty and silent, now that the livestock had run off, the pens stood with moonlight glimmering off the tops of the fence posts.

Noel approached them cautiously. Pausing to listen, he looked around.

Nothing.

"Is that Frank?" he said, feeling slightly foolish talking to thin air.

He heard a choking, bubbling cough and a weak "Help."

Noel cast caution aside. He hurried around the corrals to where the wagon stood. There, concealed in deep shadow between the wagon and fence, lay a man.

Noel stumbled over his legs and knelt beside him. "Are you Frank?" he asked. "Frank Trask?"

The man made no reply. Noel could hear his labored breathing, the rasping bubble that indicated a lung injury. He rolled the man on his side and groped across a bloody chest.

"Easy now," he said, although his heart sank with dismay. In this era of primitive medical care, he didn't think much could be done. "I'm here to help. I'm a friend."

"Ambushed—"

Violent coughing interrupted him. Noel pressed his shoulder.

"Don't talk. Save your breath. I'm going to carry you into the barn and see if I can stop the bleeding."

Frank Trask was a big man, bigger than Noel and much heavier. Noel grunted with the effort of lifting him, and for a moment as he gained his feet he thought the blood vessels in his temples would explode from the effort. Somehow he managed to stagger the short distance from the wagon to the barn.

Inside, he sank to the ground, with Frank's weight bearing him down. Shifting a sack of feed, he managed to prop the man up to help him breathe easier, and hurried off to fetch a torch.

He pulled a piece of burning lumber from the ruined bunkhouse and nearly scorched his hand in the process. Hastening back, he looked around the interior of the barn for a safe place to stand it. The barn was made of weathered lumber, warped and well dried by the harsh sun. Only its corrugated tin roof had apparently saved it from the sparks flying outside. Inside, it held stacks of emptied burlap feed sacks, loose straw, salt blocks, and a rack of dried cow hides. Everything looked inflammable.

Noel finally spotted some lanterns hanging on hooks. He lit two of these, and put out the torch by plunging it in the water trough, where it hissed noisily and sent up a gust of steam.

With light glowing through the barn, Noel set to work bandaging Frank Trask as best as he could. Rummaging through the trunks on the wagon provided him linen petticoats that he hacked into strips.

Trask's face was long and craggy, all sunburned angles in cheekbone and a big eagle nose. His mouth was a wide one, drawn now with pain. There was a gray, pallid cast to his skin beneath the tan that Noel didn't like.

Blood had soaked his entire chest. Blood was still frothing at the edges of the wound. It was close to the heart, definitely in the lung. Flecks of blood splattered Trask's lips with every labored breath. Noel bandaged him tight, trying to put a stop to the bleeding, and gave him a few sips of water. Trask swallowed some of it, but although his eyelids twitched he never regained full consciousness.

Noel covered him with another unfolded saddle blanket of Mexican wool, and sat down wearily to take stock of his two patients.

He figured the boy would be all right. One side of Cody's face was badly bruised and cut from being pistol-whipped.

But Noel doubted Frank Trask would live to see the morning.

As for the old man, riding out there in the darkness after Leon, who was crazy, mean, and lacking in conscience, well, his chances didn't look too good either.

With a sigh Noel touched the silver and turquoise cuff on his wrist.

"LOC, activate," he said.

It hummed to life, circuits shimmering through the clear sides and casting a faint glow on Noel's face.

He said, "Data query: Frank Trask, Cody Trask, and Lisa-Marie Trask. Execute."

"Working." The LOC hummed a moment, then said, "No information."

"None?" said Noel in startlement. "Is there an anomaly? Has history been changed by me or by Leon?"

"Scanning now. No information."

"Useless piece of junk," muttered Noel. With difficulty he restrained his frustration. "Okay, cross reference Double T Ranch."

"Double T Ranch . . . founded 1857 by Thomas Trask. In 1895 ownership was deeded to Don Emilio Navarres when his wife inherited it."

"Wife!" said Noel, raising his brows. "Lisa-Marie?"

"Affirmative. The ranch was added to the Navarres holdings, which encompassed an old Spanish land grant plus two hundred sections of other—"

"Stop," said Noel. "Who got the ranch after this Emilio?"

"His son, Don Esteban Navarres, who sold the land on the American side of the border in 1942 to—"

"Stop. Where does Cody come in? Why didn't he inherit the ranch?"

The LOC remained silent.

Noel frowned, thinking back over the events of today. That flash flood . . . he'd found the boy floating unconscious in the water. Maybe he *had* been intended to die by drowning. If so, had Noel himself changed history?

His mouth was suddenly very dry. He swallowed.

"Check territory birth records," he said. "Isn't there a Cody Trask registered anywhere?"

"Specific instructions are contrary."

"What?"

"Specific instructions are contrary."

"How difficult is it to scan territory birth records?" said Noel impatiently.

"Birth records registered in New Mexico territory?" said the LOC.

"Yes!" said Noel. Across the barn, Frank stirred restlessly, and Noel lowered his voice. "Yes. Territory records. Scan, dammit."

"Scanning . . . no registration."

Noel leaned back and ran his hand through his hair in frustration. "Damn," he said softly. "Damn, damn, *damn*."

He wandered outside to the trough and drank, too tired to worry about how dirty the water was. It tasted awful, like algae, but it helped fill his stomach.

The slow, steady sound of hoofbeats alerted him. He listened a moment, then returned to the barn and picked up the rifle. He thought about extinguishing the lanterns, but decided doing so would only warn the approaching rider.

Mindful of not letting himself be silhouetted against the light, Noel slipped out the back way and circled the side of the barn in the shadows. Pressing his shoulder to the rough boards, he held the rifle ready in his hands and waited.

It was a lone rider. As he crested the ridge to the north, the starry moonlight shone across his bowed head and shoulders. It looked like the old man. Noel relaxed a fraction, but he hadn't forgotten the bullet hole in his tunic. He kept himself hidden.

Trask rode into the corral and dismounted with a stagger of weariness. He stripped the saddle and bridle off his mount and gave it a halfhearted slap on the rump. The animal shook itself and drifted to the far side of the corral.

Holding his Winchester, Trask trudged to the barn. He paused at the open door, a clear target in the spill of yellow light. Then he went inside.

Noel slipped to the corner of the barn, still hugging the shadows.

From inside he heard a thump and a sorrowful "Frank! My God!"

Peering inside, Noel saw the Winchester lying on the ground. The old man knelt beside his son, gripping his hand.

Noel crept up behind Trask, making no sound until he kicked the Winchester. It went skidding across the straw. Noel pounced on it and scooped it up before the old man could struggle to his feet.

"Stay where you are," said Noel harshly. He felt slightly foolish, holding two rifles trained on an old, tear-streaked man, but the hatred burning in Trask's eyes kept him cautious.

"*You!*" said Trask furiously. "I'll—"

"You'll do nothing," said Noel. "Why did you come back?"

The fury died in the old man's eyes. His face was bleak and defeated. "Lost her. Couldn't keep the trail."

"I told you to wait until morning."

"Go to hell! I don't need your advice, you damned no good! Why don't you put a bullet in me and my boys and finish us?"

Noel lowered the rifles with a sigh. "Because, as I told you before, I am *not* your enemy. I'm a friend. At least I'm trying to be. Now, will you accept that and quit shooting at me every chance you get? Or am I going to have to tie you up?"

Trask glared at him. "I've never heard so much double-talk in all my born days. You and your Comanchero friends—"

"They are not my friends!" said Noel in exasperation. "Who do you think was out there fighting them for you? Are you blind as well as obtuse?"

"No, I ain't blind. I saw that the bastard who carried off my granddaughter is the spitting image of you. Now do you want to keep talking out of both sides of your mouth, or are you gonna be straight with me?"

Noel sighed. It seemed like he was doomed to have to explain Leon everywhere he went. Loathing went through his voice as he said, "He is my . . . twin. I don't like him. I don't claim him. I am not responsible for what he does. We are never on the same side."

The old man studied him in silence for a long while. "I reckon that's honest enough. You bandaged my boy?"

"Yes."

Trask pointed with his chin at Cody, who still slept—young and vulnerable—beneath his saddle blanket. "What about my grandson?"

"He's taken a couple of hard licks on the head today. The first was when he got caught in a flash flood."

"A flash—"

"That's right," said Noel evenly, holding the old man's eyes with his own. "I pulled him out of that before he could drown. Then he got hit again tonight. He'll have a headache when he wakes up, but otherwise he's fine."

Trask frowned and looked away. Gently he smoothed the hair back from Frank's brow. "Aw, Frank," he said in a voice that was rough with emotion. He tried to say more, then cleared his throat and struggled to his feet.

Coming over to Noel, who watched him with a mixture of compassion and wariness, he shook his head. "Frank's bad, ain't he?"

"The bullet went through his lung," said Noel. "He's lost a lot of blood."

Seen up close, Trask's eyes were a light, steely blue. They sagged with defeat. Pulling off his bandanna, he wiped his face with a hand that shook. "I reckon that's the end of him. There ain't a doctor closer than Deming, and that's a full day's ride one way."

"The bullet went out through his back," said Noel. "We don't have to worry about removing it."

Trask grunted. "No blood poisoning from that. Listen to him breathe. God have mercy, I don't think I can stand to hear him in such misery."

He looked away, his face working, then he seemed to regain control. When his gaze returned to Noel it was hard and calculating again.

"You say this outlaw that's got my gal is your brother?"

Distaste rose bitterly into Noel's mouth like bile. Unable to say the words, he nodded.

"Bad blood between you two?"

Noel nodded again. He hesitated, then said, "I'm ashamed of him."

Trask hesitated, then asked, "Will . . . will he hurt her?"

Thoughts of Elena, the beautiful wild girl of the Greek mountains, went through Noel's mind. He recalled how Leon had taken possession of her mind, how he had controlled her and brainwashed her into trying to kill Noel for him. Leon was a fragment of him, a twisted mirror image down to being right-handed and having his heart on the right side of his body. Even his name was a reversal. Noel tried to reach into his own self-knowledge, tried to think about his own flaws, his own secret though unacted-upon perversions.

"No, he won't hurt her," Noel said slowly. "Not the way you're thinking."

Trask closed his eyes. "Thank God. I been about to go out of my mind over her. We got to get her back, but how? Both Frank and Cody are hurt bad. Can you track?"

Noel blinked. "Can I what?"

"Track. You know . . . no, I guess you don't. You ain't got the least idea of what I'm talking about, do you?"

"Yes, of course," said Noel with indignation. "I'm not a moron."

"But you ain't from around here. Wearing squaw skirts and talking like an eastern greenhorn. Where're you from?"

"Chicago. A thousand years from here," said Noel bitterly. If he could have reached even the twentieth century he might have repaired his damaged LOC with the available technology. But the twenty-sixth century was as far from reach as the moon.

With an effort he recalled himself to the present and realized he had to explain himself more. "I escaped from the Indians. That's why I'm wearing . . ." Letting his voice trail off, he gestured at his torn, filthy tunic.

"You're more Cody's size than Frank's. Lisa-Marie said she'd brought Cody some new gear from Santa Fe for a gift. I reckon you could use the clothes more than him. Go ahead and dig through her things."

Noel needed no more persuasion. He went outside into the cool air and heard the coyotes yipping and howling even closer as he shouldered the carpetbags and dragged the trunk into the barn. When he'd tossed aside the tunic and stood up in the narrow canvas trousers and blue plaid shirt, he felt like a new man. The shirt would have swallowed Cody, but fit him well enough. The pants were a little short. His sunburn chafed painfully under the new clothing, but he didn't mind.

"Ain't nothing I can do about boots," said Trask. He'd soaked his bandanna in water and was busy pressing the cloth to Frank's feverish forehead.

Noel hesitated a moment, thinking about José lying dead in the back courtyard. The idea of pulling the boots off a corpse wasn't appealing, but survival was survival. He suspected the squeamish didn't last long in this country.

"I know what to do," he said. "I'll be back in a minute."

When he returned a few minutes later, Trask looked at the boots on his feet, then up at his face. He didn't say anything, and neither did Noel.

Noel stretched out, aching for sleep, and figured he could trust the old man now. Still, he kept the guns within reach.

"You take the first watch," he said. "I'll sit up with him later."

"He's my boy," said Trask grimly. "I'll do the watching."

"We'll be able to take care of tomorrow better if we both have some sleep," said Noel. "Don't let your pride get in the way of your good sense."

"You know, you got a mighty big mouth on you," said the old man. "For a greenhorn I reckon you got more sand than I figured."

Noel wasn't sure, but he thought he'd just been given a compliment. Shifting to find himself a more comfortable position on the hard floor, he said, "Yeah, well, my name, by the way, is Noel Kedran."

"Tom Trask. I put the Double T outfit together right after the Gadsden Purchase. I aim to keep it too. Ain't nobody runnin' me off my own land." He nodded at Frank. "This here's my son Frank. And that's my grandson Cody. I reckon you two already shared names if you came in together."

"We did."

"He and Lisa-Marie were my daughter's children. After Ella died, I gave 'em my name. They're Trasks, been raised Trasks, and they'll have this place after me and Frank are done with it. You got any family besides that no-count brother of yours?"

"No," said Noel.

"You got a home back East, or you just drifting?"

Noel frowned, thinking about his apartment in crowded, high-rise Chicago, thinking about the shelves stuffed with books on history and the rows of data tapes he'd recorded from his travels to ancient Greece, Rome, and Egypt. He had four rooms, a tank of tropical fish that probably needed feeding, and a neighbor with nice curves whom he'd just started getting friendly with. He wondered if his pal and fellow historian Trojan had missed him yet, if Trojan had dropped by his place to check on it. He wondered if anyone at the Time Institute was working to get him back. What, though, could they do? Two travelers could not be in the same place at the same time. They *could* send messages to him through his LOC, unless that had been damaged too by the saboteur. So far, he had received no messages.

He was alone, cut off, with no way back.

An awful loneliness rose inside him, a blackness of despair that he thrust hurriedly down. If he ever felt sorry for himself, he would be paralyzed, unable to act. He had to keep *hoping* he could find a way home.

"I guess I'm . . . drifting," he said with a catch in his voice. "Home is too far away to reach."

Trask grunted. "There're a lot of men out in this country with a past to lose. You ain't alone."

Noel thought about those words long after the lantern light had been turned low and he lay listening to the wind in the cottonwoods outside. Not alone . . . he wished it were true.

CHAPTER 4

It was like being dead among the living. He felt like a ghost, drifting without purpose, unseen, unwanted, doomed never to be a part of the lives around him.

Leon left the reins slack and allowed his mount to take him where it willed. The horse made slow though steady progress, following a dim, narrow cow track for a while, then veering off toward some low-lying hills to the south.

The sun was coming up over Leon's left shoulder, hot already although it was barely above the horizon. His hat brim provided welcome shade. He was learning he preferred the darkness; the brighter the sun the less substantial he felt, although each time he smacked his palm down upon the broad Mexican saddle horn he felt the sting of hard leather against his skin and knew that he was solid flesh and bone.

The horse picked its way up a long slope dotted with tall yucca plants. Their spears of white blooms stood in bright contrast to the cobalt sky. The morning breeze, soft and still cool, blew blossoms across the trail, raining them down upon Leon and the unconscious girl lying draped across his saddle.

He placed his hand upon the girl's back, feeling her sturdiness beneath the frilled dress she wore. She had a gathered contraption strapped onto her backside, a bustle perhaps, with a wide bow tied above it. Leon hesitated. He knew the girl was awake, but still shamming unconsciousness. He knew her mind was racing with desperation, formulating plans and discarding them. He could feel the emotions rising hot within her, anger and grief and fear all boiling for the right moment to fight back and escape.

A smile touched Leon's lips. He liked the girl's spirit. He had not yet actually entered her mind. There was no reason to do so. She was a bargaining chip for him, nothing more.

Yesterday, when he had found himself yanked abruptly to this hellish place of sand and wind-blasted scrub, it had taken forceful persuasion to convince the Comancheros to let him ride with them. He had been obliged to read their minds in order to find out where he was and in what year. At first he had thought Noel tricked him. Having promised to leave him in the town of Mistra, on the other side of the world, Noel must have intended all along to discard him here. Burning with resentment, Leon had ridden to the ranch with the other desperadoes and vented his gall by helping to destroy the place.

It wasn't until he'd seen Noel there that he realized they were indeed linked forever, like a man and his shadow, two halves of the same entity, the original and the copy. His hatred of his double burned like acid in the pit of his stomach. His only consolation was that Noel's LOC remained too damaged to let him return home. Noel was trapped, just as Leon was trapped. Two rats in the same cage.

He'd taken the girl because he knew Noel would try to save her. He'd taken the girl because El Raton—leader of the Comancheros—would enjoy using her as a hostage. She was the means by which Leon could prove his worth to the bandits. He had to belong somewhere. It might as well be with them.

Thirsty, he drew rein on top of a ridge and surveyed the parched, broken country spread out around him. Miles away, a thin spiral of smoke still rose to the sky from the burned ranch. Leon laughed softly to himself and reached for one of his canteens.

The girl pushed herself up and twisted to shove him with a hard thrust of her arms. Caught off guard, he nearly went tumbling from the saddle, and only a wrenching effort enabled him to regain his balance while she grabbed the reins and yanked the horse around in a tight circle.

He got an arm around her and clamped her close to his chest despite her wild struggles.

She jabbed him hard in the stomach with her elbow. "Let me go!"

She still had hold of the reins and was jerking them up. The horse backed and sidled, snorting uneasily. Leon did his best to pull the reins from her grasp, but she was scooting out onto the horse's neck now, leaning forward with her fingers outstretched.

Thinking she was trying to get off the horse, Leon realized too late that she was really attempting to pull off the bridle. She had it slipped forward over the horse's ears, letting it dangle across the animal's face with only the throat latch and bit to hold it on, before Leon could stop her.

"You little fool—"

He never finished his sentence. The horse put its head down and bucked. Already off balance, Leon lost his stirrups and went flying through the air. The impact with the ground drove the air from him. He lay stunned, and only the rapid sound of galloping hoofbeats roused him. Scrambling to his feet, he saw the horse run past the girl, who was standing up and gauging the distance between her and the horse intently.

As it passed her, she made a leap for the saddle horn and tried to swing herself onto the horse's back. But her long skirts hampered her. She slipped and fell flat in the dust. The horse gave a saucy flick of its tail and galloped off, the bridle still swinging and the empty stirrups flapping against its sides.

Slowly she picked herself up and slapped dust from her dress. "Stupid horse!" she shouted. "I hope you fall in a rat den and break your damn-fool leg!"

Leon stepped toward her. With a gasp she whirled around to face him and backed away. Her hair was a soft tangle of reddish gold upon her shoulders. She had an oval face, smooth pale skin beneath a pert smattering of freckles across her nose, and eyes as dark and fierce as sapphires. They flashed at Leon now.

"You keep away from me," she said. "My grandpa is going to hang you from the nearest—"

"—saguaro?" supplied Leon, amused by her spirit in spite of the trouble she'd caused.

"There are no saguaros in this country," she snapped. "A tall windmill tower will do for a hanging tree."

Leon smiled. "He has to catch me first."

"That won't be hard. You left tracks for him to follow. He's probably riding hard on our trail right now."

Leon shook his head. "No, he isn't. Look for yourself. There's no one remotely near us—"

She whirled and ran in a flurry of petticoats. Leon swore and went after her. He should have been able to catch her in a matter of seconds. But his heavy boots hampered him in the sandy ground, and she was nimble. She dodged him twice just as he was about to catch her arm, eluding him both times by a whisker.

Leon's amusement faded. It was too hot for this nonsense. He increased his speed and aimed his mind at hers, skimming the surface just enough to know which way she intended to dart next.

When she dashed around a black, thorny bush, sending jackrabbits bolting from cover, Leon dodged with her. He lunged and grabbed her arm just above the elbow.

She stopped dead in her tracks and ducked low, twisting from his grasp and doubling back. It would have worked, had he been playing fair. He again read her intentions and tackled her. His weight on top of her drove the air from her lungs. She wheezed desperately for breath, turning red, and he held her pinned.

"Now," he said, puffing for air. "You will—"

Her eyes widened at something behind him, and she screamed. It was all the warning Leon had before something round and metallic touched the back of his neck. Leon froze, his mind casting desperately. It touched nothing. From the corner of his eye he could see a man's shadow, but his mind told him nothing was there.

Spooked, he whirled, reaching for his gun. In that split second he glimpsed an Indian with stringy black hair tied back with a red headband, a dirty breechclout, and a pair of tall leather moccasins. Then the butt of the Indian's rifle connected with his chin, driving spikes of agony through his jaw and skull, and he went sprawling beside the girl.

"Pinda-lick-o-yi," said the Indian contemptuously. He was lean and honed down to a toughness unmatched by any other creature in the desert. Below the wide headband, his dark eyes were hostile. His mouth was set in a thin, cruel line.

Leon propped himself up on his elbows and again tried to touch the Indian's mind. It was as though his own reaching thought passed through air. *Nothing.*

Animal minds were dim things that he could not control,

but the Indian was completely alien. Leon felt the first stirrings of fear. He could not depend on his special abilities to get him out of this danger.

To his surprise, the girl sat up and spoke. "Apache?" she said. "Chiricahua? Mimbreños?"

The Indian shook his head. "Mescalero," he said proudly. He tapped his chest where a puckered scar ran diagonally across it. "Yotavo."

Apparently encouraged by this introduction, the girl got to her knees. "I'm Lisa-Marie Trask," she said. "Of the Double T. You've heard of my grandfather, Tom Trask. He is friends with the Apache people."

Yotavo stopped listening to her. He stepped forward and picked up a curl of her reddish-gold hair off her shoulder to study it.

Lisa-Marie shrank from him, but she forced herself not to show the throbbing fear Leon sensed in her. "Yotavo is a warrior of what clan?"

"Hair like fire," said Yotavo. He stroked her hair, then touched her cheek with his finger. Lisa-Marie jerked her head away, and the Indian smiled.

It was a cruel smile that made Leon scramble to his feet. "She's mine! Keep away from her."

Yotavo looked at him, and his gaze turned cold and hard. He raised the rifle, and Lisa-Marie stepped in front of Leon.

"Please don't kill him," she said. "Amigos. We're amigos to Yotavo."

Another Indian appeared without warning from the brush. Leading Leon's horse, he came up to Yotavo and began talking rapidly in Apache with many impatient gestures.

Leon touched Lisa-Marie's arm to get her attention. "What's the idea?" he said angrily. "I don't need your help—"

"Hush!" she whispered, her gaze locked on the two

Apaches. "I'm trying to translate what they're saying. They're talking so fast I can't be sure. It's been a long time since I heard any Apache, but I think they're arguing about El Raton and his—"

"El Raton!" said Leon loudly. He stepped forward. "Amigos," he said to the Apaches, switching to Spanish. "I am with El Raton. I helped raid the Double T Rancho last night. I am the only warrior to survive the fight. This woman is my captive."

Lisa-Marie glared at him, then swung a roundhouse punch that connected with his ear and sent him staggering. "Why, you no-good, yellow-bellied, two-faced *snake*! Do you think they care a hoot about whether you ride with El Raton or not?"

Holding his aching ear, Leon glared back at her. "I am trying to make a deal. Now, shut up—"

"Deal!" She snorted. "Yotavo and his ugly friend here would just as soon scalp you as look at you."

"Yeah? Well, whose side are you on, mine or theirs?" he retorted. "I guess you'd rather be a squaw in their camp for the rest of your life."

"I guess I wouldn't," she shot back. "At least El Raton will ransom me back to Grandpa. That's if we live long enough to get to his hideout. But you won't convince them to let us go, not the way you're going about it."

Stung by her derision, Leon said, "And just what would you suggest?"

"You—"

Yotavo pushed her to one side, holding her by the back of her neck. She started to struggle, then stood very still, her eyes a bright, frightened blue in the pallor of her face. Leon guessed Yotavo had squeezed the nerves running up the back of her neck, letting her see just a few dizzy spots as a warning to be quiet.

Yotavo spoke again in heated Apache to his friend, who grunted and shook his head. Leon figured if they continued to argue he might have a chance to...

Without warning, the second Apache swung with his war club. It connected with Leon's temple, and white rockets exploded in his skull. Through a rush of sickening agony, he felt himself topple, but darkness engulfed him before he hit the ground.

Back at the Double T, Noel was hauling up the well bucket when an unexpected wave of dizziness caught him. For a moment he fought to hang on to consciousness. The faint spell rolled away, and he found himself on his knees, clinging to the wooden water pail.

"Noel?" said Trask's gruff voice. The old man hobbled out from the charred back door of the house and gripped Noel's shoulder. "You all right?"

"Uh, yeah." Noel rubbed his face and climbed unsteadily to his feet. "I guess hunger is getting to me."

Trask's weathered face lightened with relief. "The kitchen didn't get much of the fire. It's a mess in there, but we've still got tortillas and frijoles. You finish with that water, and I'll have breakfast going before you know it."

He limped away, and Noel leaned against the plastered side of the well. The sun was coming up fast; right now it was tangled in the green branches of the cottonwoods. Soon it would be high and hot. Frank Trask was still hanging on to life by a feeble thread. Cody, looking wan and bruised, was sitting with him now.

Noel closed his eyes. He was hungry all right, but it wasn't low blood sugar that had nearly made him faint. It was Leon. He couldn't put a precise finger on the certainty growing inside him, but he suspected Leon was either injured or dead.

SHOWDOWN

Maybe Lisa-Marie had extricated herself from his clutches. Or maybe she was in even greater danger than before.

Rubbing his face again and feeling the grit of beard stubble on his jaw, Noel looked at the corral, where their lone horse stood munching on the oats Trask had put in the trough a few minutes ago. Trask was too old. Cody was still not up to par. Frank couldn't be left alone. The only one for the job was Noel.

He started for the corral, but before he'd taken two steps, a shot rang out.

Noel snatched up his Winchester, and Cody came running from the barn with the other rifle. By the time Trask had emerged from the house, Cody was halfway up the wooden windmill tower. He stared a long moment, then waved his rifle and let out a loud yell.

"Grandpa! It's Skeet, and he's bringing in the horses."

Trask glanced at Noel. "Go open the gate of the big corral, then get out of the way while he drives 'em in."

Noel obeyed. The horses came streaming in, about a dozen or so, shaking their manes and snorting. They looked as though their night on the range had done them good. Most of them went straight for the round water trough, crowding there and snapping at each other with big, yellowed teeth.

The man driving them rode into the corral, and Noel closed the gate. By the time he had it latched, the rider had stepped down from his saddle. He turned and shot Noel a measuring glance from beneath the dip of his greasy hat brim.

"Howdy," he said. His voice was low, soft, and terse.

Noel was picking up the pattern of behavior expected in this country. Without hesitation he stuck out his hand and introduced himself.

"Name's Skeet Dodd," said the cowboy. His handshake was quick and hard.

Cody came rushing up to the corral fence with a grin

splitting his face. Skeet glanced his way. "Saw the fire last night. Couldn't get here any faster."

"You sure are a sight for sore eyes," said Cody with enthusiasm. "We figure it was some of El Raton's bunch. He picked a good time to strike, with everybody gone. This here's Noel—"

"We met," said Skeet. "Where's Mr. Trask?"

"At the house, fixing breakfast. José's dead. We buried him at sunrise. Well, I—I better get back to the barn. Uncle Frank's hurt awful bad."

Cody rushed off. Skeet and Noel went through the gate together. While Noel was shutting it, Skeet resettled his hat on his head. He was as lean as leather and about Noel's age. His gunbelt hung low on a pair of slim hips, and he walked with a slow, bowlegged swagger, making soft jingles of his spur rowels with every step.

"Boy's got a hell of a black eye," he said.

"That's better than being shot," said Noel.

Skeet sent him a sharp glance. "Frank shot?"

"Through the lung. And Cody's sister has been carried off."

Skeet stopped dead. "The hell she has! Now, who—" He cut himself off, and his mouth set hard and tight. His stride lengthened, and the spurs jingled with fresh purpose. "Better get on the trail before the wind comes up and starts blowin' out the tracks."

"You've ridden all night," said Noel as they rounded the house and entered the back courtyard. "You'll be too tired to go out again—"

Skeet tugged his hat brim lower. "Nope. Mornin', Mr. Trask. I brought in the horses. Sorry I wasn't here to help."

"We're all sorry," said Trask, his voice weary. He handed over mugs of steaming coffee to each of them. "Did Noel tell you what happened?"

"Enough. Soon as I get something between my belly and my backbone, I'll saddle a fresh mount and ride."

Trask merely nodded. "We never should have let her come home. This is no place for a woman. It never was. I'll get the beans."

Noel sniffed his coffee with reluctance. It smelled strong enough to knock a man over. He sipped and grimaced at the bitter taste. When he glanced up, he found Skeet grinning at him.

"Stout enough to float a rifle cartridge," said Skeet. "Mighty fine."

Noel hated coffee. It made him think of his friend Trojan, who gulped the stuff constantly. Would he ever see the big, hairy redhead again?

The way things were going, it didn't look like it.

Fifteen minutes later, he, Skeet, and Cody mounted and rode out, heading for the low smudge of hills across the Mexican border where El Raton liked to keep his hideout this time of year. Skeet proved to be a competent tracker, silent and intent as he picked up the trail of Leon's horse.

"Got a nicked shoe on the left foreleg."

Cody's young face looked drawn and serious beneath the bruises. "We know where to find El Raton. Why don't we ride straight there? This will take too long."

Skeet rolled a plug of snuff to the other side of his jaw and spat a long stream of black tobacco juice. "Hurryin' ain't always the quickest way. We only *think* these were Raton's boys. Plenty of other Mexicans runnin' raids through this country."

Cody glanced at Noel, hesitated, then said, "They weren't Don Emilio's vaqueros, if that's what you're getting at. He and Grandpa don't get along too well, but he wouldn't burn us out."

"Son, that man's crookeder than a snattlerake, and don't

you forget it." Skeet spat again. "The only good Mexican is a dead one."

The trail went straight across the mesquite flat, easy to follow. Leon had made no attempt to conceal his tracks. His direction aimed southwest, and Skeet and Cody debated over whether he was intending to go all the way to the Animas.

The sun climbed until it blazed mercilessly and cast a shimmering heat haze over mirages of water. The country grew more barren. Greasewood was about the only vegetation in sight. Their horses kicked up a choking dust that made Noel think with longing about the water sloshing in his canteens.

Skeet drew rein abruptly, his hand in the air. "Stop and stay put," he said.

He dismounted before either Noel or Cody could ask questions. In silence they watched him walk back and forth, studying the confused mill of tracks.

Cody unstrapped his canteen from the saddle horn and took a long swig before handing it to Noel.

"Thanks." The tepid water tasted like galvanized metal, but it refreshed him nonetheless. He restricted himself to a few short sips, and handed the canteen back. "What's he looking for? The tracks keep going over there."

Skeet crouched by a set of footprints and skimmed his fingertips along them. Without answering Noel, Cody dismounted and walked over to Skeet.

"Lisa-Marie tried something, didn't she?"

Skeet grunted and walked off into the brush. He cast around for several minutes, then came back. A pink hair ribbon fluttered from his fingers.

Cody snatched it from him. "That's hers! Did she get away from him?"

"The horse," said Noel, "still went south. She wouldn't ride that way, unless she was confused about the direction."

SHOWDOWN   51

Both men shot him a scornful look.

"Lisa-Marie knows this country," said Cody. "She wouldn't get lost."

Skeet wandered off again. This time, when he returned, his face looked grim. "The horse went south, then it doubled back. Look here."

Cody followed him, and Noel dismounted to do the same. About ten yards or so from where they left their horses, they found a small clearing in the greasewood where the dirt was scuffed and gouged. The tracks were confused and indistinct. Skeet pointed to a set of blurred ones, almost indistinguishable.

Cody turned pale. " 'Paches! How many?"

"Just one, I think. Maybe two, but they didn't stay together." Skeet took off his hat to wipe out the inside. His forehead had a pronounced tan line about halfway up from his brows—dark and weathered below, pale up toward his hairline.

"You think he caught them?" asked Cody anxiously.

"Not much of a fight either," said Skeet, putting on his hat again. "No spent cartridge shells. No blood."

Cody turned away and stared blindly in the direction of the ranch. "If—if he was going to scalp them, he'd have done it already. Wouldn't he?"

"Maybe. They take prisoners sometimes."

"Maybe Leon took the Apache prisoner," said Noel. He knew his duplicate had advantages these men knew nothing about. It would be difficult if not impossible to sneak up unawares on Leon. It would be hard to beat him in a fight.

Skeet looked at him with eyes like stone. "You loco or just gone from sunstroke?"

Noel's temper flared. "Look, I happen to know Leon better than either of you—"

"Grandpa said you two are the spitting image of each

other," broke in Cody. "Are you twins?"

Noel scowled. "Yes. That's—"

"Just like me and Lisa-Marie! Only we aren't identical. Do you know what he's thinking sometimes? Do you—"

Skeet drew his pistol and aimed it at Noel. "Shut up, Cody."

Noel's gut tightened. He felt cotton-mouthed and exasperated at having to explain himself all over again. "There's no need for the gun."

"I'll judge. If you're friends with the Comancheros, you turned up awful coincidental like."

"No, he didn't!" said Cody, stepping between Skeet and Noel. Swiftly he did the explaining, finishing with, "Now, he's been good help when we needed it most. Back off, Skeet, and put your gun away. We can't help Lisa-Marie if we keep wasting time like this."

Skeet didn't look convinced, but he holstered his gun. Noel eased out the breath he'd been holding.

"Thanks, kid," Noel said, keeping his gaze on Skeet. "Now, would you please explain why you think the Indian has them instead of the other way around?"

In silence Skeet led him to where the horse tracks headed east. Two sets of footprints followed the hoofprints. Skeet held up two fingers in a V. "White men walk this way. Heels in, toes out. Indian footprints go parallel. Now look at that track right there and tell me that ain't a woman's."

The print was small and narrow. Noel frowned at it, remembering his brief dizzy spell early this morning. That must have been when the Indian jumped Leon.

"He's got 'em tied up and walking," said Skeet. "He'll walk 'em all day, and pretty soon he'll pull the shoes on that horse. Then he'll cover his trail. If he goes up into the rocks, we'll never find them."

"We've *got* to," said Cody angrily. "I'm not leaving Lisa-

SHOWDOWN

Marie in the hands of a bunch of dirty, no-good 'paches. Let's ride!"

They swung into their saddles, the leather seats scorching hot with reflected heat. Gathering his reins, Noel looked south and saw an approaching cloud of dust. He pointed.

"More trouble?" he asked.

"Oh, damnation!" said Cody. "That much dust means a lot of riders. If it's soldiers, Noel, don't you dare say one word about my sister or the 'paches."

Noel blinked in surprise. "But why not? Surely we could use the help."

"No!"

Skeet turned on him fiercely. "Soldiers get wind of captives and they blunder in. The captives end up dead, every time."

"But—"

"We can get her back," said Cody breathlessly, his freckles standing out. "But it takes ransom—trading ponies or cattle in exchange. Soldiers will attack, and the Indians will kill her."

"I understand," said Noel.

Cody shot him a grateful look, but Skeet scowled.

"You'd better," he said in a low voice of warning. "Or you won't see another sunrise."

"Skeet!" said Cody. "He said he understood."

Skeet spat tobacco. "Said it. Didn't say he'd be quiet. All we need is some tenderfoot from back East who thinks he knows how to run everybody's business—"

"I give you my word," snapped Noel.

Skeet stared at him a long time. Noel met his gaze angrily, not flinching, not evading.

"Don't push him, Skeet," said Cody.

"He's pushing me," said Skeet, but he dropped the staring match and wheeled his horse around to face the riders.

CHAPTER 5

∞

The argument proved unnecessary, for the riders turned out to be twenty or so vaqueros in big sombreros, Mexican cowboys in short jackets and dark mustaches, their eyes like black flint, their faces hostile.

In the lead rode a broad-shouldered man with keen hazel eyes beneath drooping lids, and an aristocratic European face. Thick brown hair curled beneath his flat-crowned hat. Embossed silver decorated his saddle and bridle, flashing in the sun. Long leather *tapederos* covered his stirrups, the tips almost brushing the ground. Silver conchas flashed from them as well, twinkling just above the scruffy broomweed as he reined in his prancing black stallion with a flourish and a wave of his quirt.

"Greetings, señors," he said cheerfully. His voice was like cream, warm and rich with the flavor of a Mexican accent. He swept Noel and Skeet with a single glance, and focused his gaze on the boy. "Cody, how is your grandfather? One of my men came in last night, telling of a fire in your direction. I hope it was not your ranch, but this morning I could not enjoy the singing of the birds in my garden because of worry, and so I have come to see if there is help I can give."

"Howdy, Don Emilio," said Cody. "It was our ranch. Raton's bunch tried to burn us out."

"That *diablo*!" said Don Emilio, but mildly. "Was anyone hurt?"

Cody squinted, and the harsh sunlight picked out the strain in his young face. "Yes, sir. My uncle got shot bad. We don't know if he'll make it. They carried off my sister—"

A stir went through the vaqueros. Don Emilio dropped his urbane mask. His gaze grew sharp and intent. "This is very bad," he said. "You will please explain to me all that has happened."

"While we're jawin'," broke in Skeet impatiently, "that Apache is gettin' farther off."

Noel glared at him. After his big production of keeping the facts about the Indian quiet, here Skeet was, shooting off his mouth. It didn't figure.

Don Emilio's eyes went again to each of their faces. "What Apache?"

Cody frowned, his face mirroring the exasperation Noel felt. He said, "One Comanchero got her. The rest are locked up in our saddle house. We tracked them this far, but it looks like they got bushwhacked by a 'pache."

Don Emilio looked very grave. The gloved hand holding his reins tightened into a fist. "Some renegade Chiricahuas are said to be heading our way from Sonora, but I do not think they have come this far east. The Mescaleros have been stealing my cattle all spring. It could be a warrior from Tonithian's clan, or it could be Kansana."

Abruptly he turned in the saddle and addressed his vaqueros in rapid Spanish. Noel's LOC, acting as a translator, supplied meaning to his words. " . . . the mountains and bring El Raton to the hacienda. Pedro, ride straight to Palomas and take the doctor to the Double T. The rest of you, go there now and assist the old man. Obey his orders as you would mine."

Two thirds of the riders galloped off toward the mountains. The rest started northeast, toward the ranch. Don Emilio smiled at Cody. "Let us investigate this matter of an Indian who dares too much. I am at your disposal, señors."

Cody smiled. "That's real neighborly—"

"We don't need your help," said Skeet.

The warmth chilled slightly in Don Emilio's eyes. "I think you do," he said pleasantly. "None of you speaks Apache. Do you expect to bargain for her in bits of broken Spanish and English? Let us go, amigos."

"Not so fast!" said Skeet. "Where're you sending those men?"

"To help Trask," said Noel before Don Emilio could answer.

The grandee's hazel eyes reappraised him. "You speak Spanish, señor?"

"Yes. But why didn't you keep some of your men with us? The more we have, the better we can—"

"No," said Don Emilio firmly, "that is untrue. You do not understand the hatred between Apaches and Mexicans, I think. The señorita will be safer if four brave men ask for her return."

Skeet snorted. "He means a Mex army would get her killed sure."

"Or start a little war," said Don Emilio.

"I see," said Noel. "Well, thanks for sending the doctor. The old man will be grateful."

Cody's blue eyes widened. "You're sending a doctor to help Uncle Frank?"

Don Emilio shrugged. "It is the least I can do, no? If his wound is truly serious, perhaps help will come too late. But I know your grandfather well enough to think he has not sent for the gringo physician in Deming."

"No," said Cody. "It's too far, and we couldn't spare the rider."

"My man is closer. And now, for your sister—"

"We'll find her without your help," said Skeet. "The only folks who hate Mexicans more than I do are Indians. You go riding into their camp, and they'll kill her sure."

Don Emilio's expression grew still and cold. "You are mistaken, my friend. I am known by these bands. We have talked many times."

"So you're friends?" Skeet spat tobacco scornfully. "Just like you're friends with those Comancheros. My, ain't you bein' helpful all of a sudden. And here I figured you were payin' El Raton and his boys to steal our cattle and burn our ranch. Mr. Trask sittin' home couldn't put up much fight if your vaqueros are aimin' to finish off the job."

"Skeet!" said Cody in anger. "Shut up—"

"The hell I will," said Skeet. "He ain't no—"

Noel's fist connected with Skeet's jaw with a thud that jolted his hand to the wrist and sent the cowboy sprawling to the ground. By the time Skeet scrambled furiously to his feet, spurs jingling and dust fogging around him, Noel had dismounted.

Skeet's hand went for his gun, but Noel stepped in close with a quick one-two punch that snapped back Skeet's head and sent him reeling against his horse. The animal shifted away, snorting. Regaining his balance, Skeet turned around. He'd lost his hat. Blood trickled from the corner of his mouth, and his eyes were flat and mean.

Noel swung again, but this time Skeet dodged the blow and delivered a roundhouse punch that made stars explode across Noel's vision. He shook his head to clear it and ducked another swing, coming up under Skeet's arm and using the man's own impetus to throw him down.

Skeet lay there on his back, winded and stunned. When

he got up a second time, he did so slowly. He dabbed at the blood on his mouth, but he made no attempt to continue the fight.

Breathing heavily, Noel said, "I don't understand why you say one thing and do another, but from where I come from, that's suspicious. Why don't you stop causing trouble and let us get on with finding the girl?"

Noel turned to pick up his horse's reins. From the corner of his eye he saw Skeet reach for his gun. Noel whirled to face him, his heart hammering fast, but a sharp click came from behind him and Don Emilio said, "I do not think you should draw, amigo. If you do, I will have to shoot you in the hand. Sometimes my aim is not so good, and I hit people in the chest or the stomach or that place in the thigh where the artery pumps *mucho* blood. Why don't you be very still and save us trouble?"

Red-faced, Skeet dropped his hand away from the butt of his pistol.

"Get on your horse and ride!" said Cody. His voice cracked on him, and that seemed to make him even angrier. "Right now! Get on back to the ranch and help Grandpa!"

Skeet stared at him in consternation. "You ain't goin' off with these two?"

"Yes, I am, and the sooner you get out of our way the sooner we can catch up with Lisa-Marie."

"Now, boy," said Skeet sharply. "You think about what you're doing. Navarres is trying his best to take the Double T away from your grandpa, and this here stranger is likely helping him."

"Not likely," said Noel quietly.

"Cody!" said Skeet. "We're pals, boy. You can't side with them against me."

Cody's face twisted with indecision. "You're making this awful hard. It ain't one side against the other. They're the only help we've got, and right now we need them."

"Thought you and me were saddle pals," said Skeet.

"You're playing head games with the boy," said Noel. "Stop it."

"Are you gonna ride on back to the ranch like I said?" asked Cody. "Or—"

"I take my orders from Mr. Trask," said Skeet in a low, tight voice. "He said to bring his girl home. I aim to do it."

"Not with us, I think," said Don Emilio.

Noel was still standing by his horse's head. He took a quick step toward Skeet, who backed up involuntarily, then caught himself with a scowl.

"You think you've whipped me, tenderfoot, but you ain't," he said.

"Ride," said Noel.

"I'm the best tracker this side of El Paso," said Skeet.

Cody hesitated. His eyes sought first Don Emilio's, then Noel's.

Noel said, "I can find her."

Skeet laughed harshly. "*You?* How?"

"I can find Leon," said Noel, not intending to explain how he could set the directional locator on his LOC and go straight to Leon. "As long as she's with him—"

"That's crazy!"

"No, it's not," said Cody eagerly. "They're twins, same as me and Lisa-Marie are twins. When we were little, sometimes I could tell what she was going to say before she said it. She was better at figuring me out than I was her. I got lost once while we were playing in Silver Canyon, and she found me. I'll bet Noel can find his brother."

Without another word Skeet picked up his greasy hat and crammed it on his head. He swung aboard his horse. "If she turns up dead, with her scalp hanging on the lodge pole, don't blame me."

No one answered him, and he lashed his horse on the flank, riding away at a furious gallop.

Noel watched him go for a couple of seconds, then turned his head and caught Don Emilio staring at him intently. The Mexican smiled, but it never reached his intelligent hazel eyes.

Noel didn't smile back. He climbed onto his horse and tapped Cody on the shoulder.

The boy was looking worried, but he managed a lopsided grin for Noel. "I guess we shouldn't have run him off. He is the best tracker around. Uncle Frank will sure be mad at me if Skeet quits the Double T." Cody's voice broke. For a moment his toughness vanished and he was just a scared, upset kid.

He gulped a little, and Noel put his hand on the boy's shoulder in silent reassurance. "You made the right decision," he said.

"I hope so," said Cody. He looked at Don Emilio, who was watching them like a cat at a mousehole. "What he said was true. You and Grandpa ain't exactly friends."

"Neither are we enemies," said Don Emilio smoothly. "While we talk the day grows longer. Shall we ride?"

He cast about until he picked up the trail left by the Apache and his two captives. "He is heading toward those hills. Kansana is camped there," said Don Emilio.

Cody turned pale. "We've got to hurry! We've got to get her back before—"

Noel gripped the boy's arm. "Easy. Hysterics won't help."

"He is not many hours ahead of us, this brave," said Don Emilio, spurring his horse forward. The stallion reared and tried to leap into a gallop. Don Emilio controlled him, reining him to a fast, ground-eating trot. "He must go slowly, because they are walking behind his horse. We can catch up before they reach Kansana's camp."

"I thought you said you were on good terms with Kansana,"

said Noel. He didn't like the fear in Cody's eyes. It was the naked, desperate kind, the ratlike, scrambling kind. The boy wasn't thinking; he was just reacting. That was dangerous. "Don Emilio? Didn't you say—"

"*Sí,* I know him," said Don Emilio impatiently. "Good friends? No. That is not possible with the Apache."

"Kansana doesn't keep white captives," muttered Cody. His hands were tight on the reins, and his horse was tossing its head as though picking up the emotions in its rider.

"I don't understand," said Noel. "Why take them in, if—"

"It is a very great coup," said Don Emilio with a flash of white teeth, although he did not look amused. "The Comanchero will die. The girl . . . probably they will trade her to another band. *But,*" he added with emphasis, glancing at Cody who looked like he might throw up at any moment, "this will not be her fate. We are going to rescue her first, amigos."

In the powdery dirt the trail was easy to follow. Even Noel could make out the hoofprint with the nicked shoe. Two parallel sets of footprints were spaced on either side of the hoofprints, indicating that Leon and Lisa-Marie were walking side by side. The girl's tracks showed small square heels and very pointed toes. Noel tried to envision female footgear of the late Victorian period. His mental memory banks conjured up a vague idea of high-topped button shoes, very narrow and high-heeled. If Lisa-Marie were walking in shoes like that, her feet would soon be in agony.

As for Leon, he should have been able to pull one of his mental hypnosis tricks on the Indian by now. He must be injured, but if he was hurt badly he wouldn't be able to walk far.

Now and then the tracks were blurred, betraying where one or both of the captives had stumbled. Don Emilio reined to a halt and pointed at a wide drag mark.

"The man fell, and was dragged through the mesquite. Ah, *sí*, I am right. Here is part of his shirt and some of his trousers." The scraps of fabric caught on long, wicked thorns fluttered in the dry, hot wind blowing from the west.

Past the mesquite thicket, Leon's tracks reappeared, indicating that he had regained his feet. Now and then the footprints wavered. Leon was dragging one foot. Lisa-Marie stumbled often.

Overhead, the sun blazed like a furnace. The wind gave no relief. Noel's mouth felt so dry he couldn't work up enough spit to swallow. He took small, careful sips of the tepid water from his canteen, making the precious liquid last. What sufferings of thirst the captives must be going through, he didn't want to consider.

Don Emilio reined up again. "He has pulled off the shoes."

"Aw, damn!" said Cody, wiping his face with his arm. "Now we're really gonna be—"

"Who pulled off his shoes?" asked Noel, coming up last. "Leon?"

Only then did he see the four iron horseshoes lying scattered on the ground. He felt like a fool for having asked such an ignorant question, and his face heated up beneath the scorn in Cody's eyes.

Don Emilio's lips quirked slightly, but he said nothing. The soft ground grew harder and stonier. Patches of tall, tan grass rippled in the wind and yucca plants stood loaded with snowy blooms. Pack rats, plump and anxious, scurried across their trail to vanish into dens dug beneath bushes with long, dull green needles.

Maintaining his place at the rear, Noel gradually fell farther and farther back. Bringing his wrist surreptitiously to his mouth, he whispered in the directions for a locator sweep. It didn't take a genius to figure that as soon as they reached the rocky foothills, they were going to lose the trail. Already

Don Emilio had slowed their pace. His dark head swiveled constantly as he rode. His gaze swept the ground, pausing where the tracks vanished, only to find them again a few feet onward.

"LOC, confirm locator command," whispered Noel.

"Confirm," replied the LOC.

Cody glanced back at him and waved.

Noel rubbed his jaw with his wrist and lowered his arm, feeling his heart going absurdly fast.

Cody waved again, signaling for him to catch up. Noel kicked his horse, and it broke into a lope until it reached Cody's mount.

"You gotta stay with us," said Cody.

Noel glanced back the way they'd come and saw a faint speck through the heat waves shimmering on the horizon. A faint speck throwing up dust.

"What's that?" he asked.

Cody frowned, flushing bright red. He glanced back quickly and shrugged. "I don't see nothing."

"Sure you do, eagle-eye," said Noel. "Is Skeet following us?"

Cody shrugged again. "It could be someone out looking for his lost cow."

Don Emilio wheeled his horse around to face them. Dust had powdered his face and clothing. "What is that so charming expression of you Americano cowpunchers? If a frog could fly, he would not bump his tail every time he jumped? We are not on your grandfather's land, Cody. I do not think he runs his cattle this far. My men are branding south of the hacienda today. I think we must say that it is Skeet."

Cody turned even redder. "He's crazy."

"He's trouble," said Noel.

Don Emilio sighed. "I think he may be useful. I have lost the trail."

CHAPTER 6

∞

A full moon floated in the sky, casting down light strong enough to read by. Noel's shadow extended ahead of him as he slipped away from the sleeping camp nestled in the curve of a shallow canyon.

The air was cold and still, hushed like a pent breath. Around Noel rose sky and mountain, bigger than life, dwarfing him to an insignificant speck, all in varying shades of black and gray like a washed pen and ink drawing. He smelled dust on the crisp, clean air and the acrid scent of weeds crushed beneath his boot soles as he walked.

The climb was steep enough to make him puff by the time he reached the top of the canyon. He paused to catch his breath and stared down at his companions rolled in their saddle blankets around a dead campfire. The scent of wood ash spiraled up now and then, ghostly faint.

Noel had first watch. He figured sentry duty could take a rest for a while. A consultation with his LOC was long overdue, but this was the first privacy he'd had all day.

In the distance an owl hooted. Nervous prickles ran up the

back of his neck. He shoved his fingers through his hair and activated the LOC.

The shape of the turquoise and silver cuff changed from a primitive artifact to a sophisticated technological wonder. A dim shimmer of light from its pulsing circuitry shone through the clear sides of the bracelet. Biochips of microscopic size, miniaturized circuits, and fiber optics—all the miracles of twenty-sixth-century technology—were useless junk as long as the damage went unrepaired.

He sighed. If he could reach the twenty-first century, even the twentieth, the necessary tools would be available to him. But in this time, telegraph wire was about the most sophisticated form of communication in existence. If he caught a stagecoach or train back East, he might find a telephone, but it would be too crude to help him jury-rig repairs.

"LOC, run diagnostic codes," he said.

"Running."

"Locate malfunction."

The LOC pulsed steadily.

"Well?" said Noel impatiently. "Have you located it?"

"Affirmative."

"And it is?"

"Closed time loop. Recall canceled. Communication sending canceled. Emergency recall canceled. Destination codes . . . destination codes . . . destination codes—"

"Stop!" he said, afraid the computer might burn itself out. "Well, I guess I'd already guessed as much, but it's so nice to have it verbally confirmed."

"Is that a question?" asked the LOC.

"No."

He rubbed his eyes, which were gritty from lack of sleep. His face and hands hurt from sunburn. His rump ached from hours in the saddle. His knees felt permanently bowed. His mouth was so dry, he wondered if he would ever find enough water to drink again. He stank of dried sweat and dust. Beard stubble made his jaw itch.

He scratched, trying not to give way to irritation and fear. He'd spent most of his visit to medieval Greece battling those two emotions, reacting in panic, and hauling himself out of crisis after crisis. But now, he was beginning to accept the fact that he couldn't get back. Not accept it as in give up hope, but accept it to the point that he could try to adapt.

"LOC," he said, "is self-repair possible?"

"Negative."

"Find parameters. Specifically: Is safety-chain programming still operational? Can safety-chain programming be shut off? Can destination and time codes be set at will? Or are those codes on random placement? Run."

"Running ... safety chain is operational. It cannot be canceled. Destination codes ... destination codes ... destination—"

"Stop!"

Frowning, Noel hugged his knees against his chest in a futile attempt to stay warm while he considered his options. Right now, they looked unappealing.

Travel operated on a forty-nine to one ratio, with forty-nine minutes of travel time equal to one minute of normal time. Usually a normal research mission took place in about one and a half days of travel time, and then the traveler returned home with his data and recordings. If something went wrong, say a LOC was lost or removed from the traveler's possession for a short time, then the safety-chain program was designed to build in a longer stay in the past by adding tiny time loops within the original one. Noel's LOC was programmed with three safety chains, with each chain lasting about twelve hours in travel time. At the end of the chain, he was either yanked home or he had to stay forever in the era he was visiting. Any alterations to history would become permanent, and the time-paradox principle would go into effect.

Now, although it seemed he could never return to the Time Institute, or to his home, friends, and fellow historians, he still had to contend with the fact that he wouldn't be allowed to stay here permanently either. Safety chain would yank him out, sooner or later, to drop him elsewhere. His LOC was telling him there was nothing he could do about it.

Even throwing the LOC away was an option denied him. He had an implant that conditioned him to never let the LOC willingly out of his possession.

Noel stared around at the bleak night landscape. Stars dappled the sky. The jutting mountains, the deep gash of canyon, the tumbled thrust of boulders . . . the silence, the emptiness, the loneliness.

He shivered. It was an alien land. He might as well have been sitting on Mars, for all the comfort he found here. By training and inclination, he felt comfortable in Rome, among the legions of her army, or garbed in toga and sandals, speaking the heavy Latin phrases. He felt comfortable among the Greeks of legend, scrambling over mountains rich with honey and almonds, a wineskin slung over his shoulder and a bow in his hand. If he had to live in a desert, let him live among the pyramids, where bewigged officials in linen gauze and gold collars drove their chariots at breakneck pace along the banks of the Nile.

He did not belong here in this bleak land of rattlesnake and scorpion, this land of gun and arrow. Men were too few. The only law was survival. Death came from animals, snakes, insects, sudden flood, or gradual dehydration. Death came from other men—white or Indian made little difference.

This was a land of silence. Men talked little, too beaten by the merciless sun and heat, too aware of the need to conserve life.

"LOC," he said, "how much time remaining in this location?"

"Unknown."

"What do you mean, unknown? I've been here a day and a half already—"

"Thirty-two hours, fifteen minutes—"

"Stop. How many more hours before the safety chain yanks me out of here?"

"Unknown."

"You have to know. Run diagnostics."

"Running . . . Anomaly warning."

"What? Oh, hell. What has Leon done?"

Noel asked the question, but he already knew the answer. Before the LOC could reply, he said, "I know. He kidnapped Lisa-Marie Trask. I'd like to know how long I've got to find her and get her home to her folks before my time runs out."

"Anomaly warning."

He sighed, trying to put a lid on his impatience. "Specify."

"Actions to change history have already occurred."

"I *know* that, you piece of junk. I saved Cody's life and Leon carried off Lisa-Marie. Are you trying to tell me that she dies? Is she killed by the Indians? Relate specific history of Trask family."

The LOC remained silent.

Alarmed, Noel said sharply, "Are you malfunctioning?"

"Negative."

"Relate specific history of Trask family."

"No data."

"Wait a minute. You had data before. You told me that Lisa-Marie inherits the old man's ranch and she marries Don Emilio, who then ends up with the place. I don't know why anyone would want a piece of ground that looks like this, but everyone here seems possessive."

"Rhetorical," said the LOC.

"No, I'm not being rhetorical," retorted Noel. "I'm asking for data. Spit it out."

"Parallel history alternatives. Anomaly warning. No data."

Noel chewed on that a moment, fighting off a growing sense of dismay. "You mean we've messed up history again."

"Affirmative."

"Damn."

Noel thought about how they'd spent the last couple of hours of daylight casting about fruitlessly for the tracks. It was as though Lisa-Marie and Leon had vanished into thin air. The trail was gone, and although Don Emilio searched for bent weeds, horse droppings, even a scuff on the ground, there was nothing. The dirt here in the foothills was stone hard and littered with shale that shifted and crunched underfoot. No tracks showed on it, not even their own. Of course the LOC's directional finder could scan for Leon. But when Noel had pointed at the mountains looming above them, Don Emilio had slapped the dust wearily from his hat and suggested that they camp for the night.

Skeet had veered off and vanished once they spotted him. Noel didn't like him hanging around somewhere out in the dark, but there wasn't anything they could do about it. Don Emilio seemed nervous. He said they were close enough to attract the notice of Apache scouting parties. He'd let them have a fire just long enough to burn the rabbit he shot, then the ashes had been smothered with dirt.

The owl hooted again. Maybe it had lost its roost.

Reluctantly Noel went back to his questions. "So we've changed history. What happens if we don't change it back?"

The LOC hummed for a while.

Remembering how fast it used to function before it was

sabotaged, Noel gnawed on his lip and tried to be patient. They used to be a smooth team. He'd even been considered one of the top historians in the travel department. He had empathy with his specialty area. He never failed to bring back useful, often unusual data.

Had they figured out yet at the Institute that they'd lost him? he wondered. Did they care?

"LOC, reply to question," he said. "What happens if we don't change history back?"

Something tapped him on the shoulder. His heart shot into his throat, and he whirled around.

A shadowy figure stood before him, a figure lean and straight, clad in a breechclout that hung to his knees. The moonlight glinted off the tip of an arrow nocked back and aimed at Noel's heart.

He froze, his heart pounding. The LOC glowed on his wrist, casting an eerie light over the ground.

I never heard him, Noel thought furiously to himself. "LOC, deactivate. Disguise mode," he said swiftly.

The LOC's circuits dimmed, and it shimmered briefly on his wrist as it resumed its shape of silver and turquoise.

The Indian's bow and arrow lowered slightly. "Power maker," he whispered in awe. "Much Power."

He spoke in Apache, but Noel's translator handled it. Eager to snatch any advantage given, Noel said, "Yes, I possess much power. You have disturbed me. Go away."

"All clan leaders have a Power," said the Indian. His eyes shifted like liquid darkness in the moonlight. "Kansana has Power over rattlesnakes. They do not bite him, and his touch can cure others of the venom. I am Tahzi, his son. Someday I will be a clan leader too. What is your Power?"

For a moment Noel was afraid the Indian might throw a snake on him to see what would happen. "If you do not recognize my Power," he said with all the arrogance he could muster, "then I cannot speak of it to you. It is not discussed. You have seen it, and that is enough."

The Indian stared at him for what seemed like an eternity, then he turned away.

Noel took a quick half step after the man and said, "Wait! We are looking for an Apache brave who has taken two white captives. A man and a girl. Are these captives in Kansana's camp?"

The brave scowled. "We do not take slaves from the Pinda-lick-o-yi."

"Someone has taken them. We have been following their trail all day. Has another band of Apaches camped in these hills?"

"Some Tchiene," said Tahzi with scorn. "An old man and three toothless women."

Noel frowned. He didn't think an old man could capture Leon. "The girl is the granddaughter of Tom Trask. He will pay a large ransom for her safe return."

"I know nothing of this girl," said the brave flatly. "Ransom is a matter for Kansana to decide."

What did that mean? Noel wondered. White men might have the reputation for double-talk, but this character was as slippery as they came.

"I'd like to speak to Kansana," he said. "Would it be possible for me to go to his camp? Would you take me there?"

"Ask your Power these questions," said Tahzi with scorn. "Kansana does not speak to a White Eyes."

"But—"

The Apache turned and melted soundlessly into the shadows. Noel hesitated only a couple of seconds. He thought the Indian was lying about Leon and Lisa-Marie. Although he could follow the directional on his LOC in the morning, he had serious doubts now about the wisdom of riding any closer to the Apache camp in broad daylight. Scouts would alert the camp, and Leon and Lisa-Marie could be killed quickly.

Maybe it was time to do a little sneaking around himself.

Reluctant to desert his sleeping companions, he couldn't afford to waste the time telling them his plan. Besides, with some luck, he might be back by daylight.

"LOC," he whispered, "activate a directional sweep. Is Leon's location in the same direction the Indian is going?"

"Affirmative."

"Maintain disguise mode," said Noel. "Extend electromagnetic field, human body level, around me. Guide me by pulse code. Voice activation off."

The LOC acknowledged by emitting a single warm pulse against his wrist. Noel set off after Tahzi, following him at a prudent distance, and keeping to all the cover available. He wasn't certain the electromagnetic field would work as a true shield, especially since the Apache's survival senses were so sharply attuned to his environment, but it was worth a try.

After a mile or two, Noel relaxed a fraction, deciding the Apache wasn't going to circle back and ambush him. The trail grew steeper and more treacherous. A thin layer of cirrus clouds obscured the moon. Coyotes wailed in the distance, making Noel shiver.

He topped a ridge and crouched low to keep himself off the skyline. The Apache ahead couldn't be seen, but the LOC was still pulsing steadily against his wrist so Noel wasn't worried about losing him.

Then Tahzi veered off the trail. Whether he was hunting or circling back, Noel couldn't tell. He decided he didn't want to find out. Swiftly he left the trail and scooted his way down a steep slope of juniper and rock to a hollow of concealment deep in the shadows between two boulders. He pressed his shoulders tight against the rock and held his breath.

After a few seconds, he heard a faint scuff of moccasined

feet over rock. Glancing up, he saw Tahzi pass by on the mountain trail, illuminated briefly in the moonlight. Noel froze, his heart whamming in a harsh rhythm. The Indian didn't detect his presence, didn't falter. Within seconds, the brave vanished from sight.

Maybe he was going back to scalp Don Emilio and Cody, sleeping without a sentry to warn them of attack. Noel felt guilty about that, but he squelched the feeling and climbed back to the trail.

Within another hour he crawled on his belly over an escarpment of cold stone and peered down into a canyon divided by a rushing mountain stream. Indian wickiups stood scattered about on the level ground, looming large and indeterminate in the shadows. The moon had vanished; it was hard to see anything.

Patience wasn't one of Noel's best traits. But he forced himself to lie there and keep quiet. There had to be scouts posted about the camp for protection. He didn't want to encounter one and end up with his throat cut and his scalp lifted.

The camp smelled faintly of ashes, horse dung, and untanned leather. Across the canyon a bird twittered sleepily from a juniper thicket, then burst into sweet, piercing song. A trio of hunters armed with bows and arrows came into camp, one bearing a deer across his shoulders. He threw it down, and his companions knelt at the stream to drink thirstily.

Watching, Noel licked his dry lips. The very bubble and murmur of the stream tormented him with thirst. He was hungry, for he'd barely eaten any of the stringy rabbit they'd had for supper. Right now, venison looked tasty.

The captives weren't in sight. As he waited he tried to think of a plan. All he had was a pistol and a handful of bullets. The last thing he meant to do was start shooting at sunrise. It would be better to scoot back to Don Emilio and get reinforcements, but first he needed definite proof that the captives were alive and well.

One of the hunters thrust aside a door flap and crawled into a wickiup. The others flopped down on the ground near their kill and slept there like dogs.

By the time the sun finally came up, Noel was bleary-eyed and tired of lying on the cold ground with his face being scratched by sticker weeds. A scorpion crawled over his fingers, its yellow tail curled over its back, and Noel barely kept himself from flinching.

Below, the camp stirred and came to life. Soon cooking fires were sending up tempting aromas. Brown, sturdy children scampered in play. A pair of squaws dragged the deer off into the shade of some mesquite trees and began skinning it. Their laughing chatter drifted up to Noel.

He frowned, his gaze searching among the half-dozen wickiups and beyond. No sign of captives. No evidence of people being tortured. No moans for mercy. No cries for help. No long reddish-blond scalps hanging from the lodge pole.

For the first time Noel allowed himself to doubt his LOC. Just about everything else on it was malfunctioning. Maybe the directional locator was too. This could be a major wild goose chase.

With a sigh he decided to get closer, when female shrieks rent the air and one of the wickiups rocked. Women kneeling at metates, grinding dried mesquite beans into flour, paused in their work. Others put down the moccasins they were making or stopped filling pitch-coated water baskets. Children gathered swiftly. Even some of the men strolled over.

The wickiup rocked again. Sounds of violent argument punctuated by screaming rose in the air. Someone laughed. Then without warning the door flap flew aside, and two figures locked together in mortal combat came rolling out. Both women were scratching, pulling hair, gouging, kicking, and yelling curses. They went over and over in a wild tangle, stirring up dust and scattering the onlookers.

It wasn't until then that Noel got a clear look at them. He realized that one of the women had red-gold hair. At once he stiffened, his interest intent. It had to be Lisa-Marie, and she was winning the battle.

By now she was on top and had her opponent pinned. She slapped away the brown hands reaching for her throat and landed a punch that her brother must have taught her. The Apache woman gave up, coughing and spitting, and Lisa-Marie scrambled to her feet. She bolted for freedom like a gazelle, her pale slender legs a blur of moccasins under the beaded leather skirt.

One of the braves, a bronzed youth with a scarlet cloth twisted about his black hair, went after her. She ran with the speed of desperation, not bothering to glance back. She almost reached the edge of the canyon, but the brave's easy lope was faster.

He caught her by the hair, giving a swift, harsh yank that pulled her off balance and sent her sprawling at his feet. She yelled at him and tried to scramble away, but he planted a moccasin on her shoulder.

Lisa-Marie threw her arm across her face and sobbed. The brave bent and slipped a leather noose about her slender throat. He tugged lightly, then harder as she ignored him. With a growl, he gripped her arm and pulled her to her feet. He spoke roughly to her, shaking the end of the leather thong in her face in admonition. Lisa-Marie stood with her head averted. Dirt was smeared across the fine beadwork of the leather dress she wore. Her bare arms gleamed white and vulnerable in the sunshine.

The brave led her back to the center of the camp and tied her to a stake driven in the ground. The children circled her, jeering.

Noel decided he'd seen enough. He wasn't going to leave without her. She was brave and a fighter, but they might kill her at any moment.

Drawing his pistol, Noel slithered back off the escarpment and turned around. He made his way to the trail, keeping to cover and trying to make no sound in the rocks. He was way too close to the camp, and now it was broad daylight.

The sun wasn't hot yet, but he was sweating heavily.

Ahead, he could see a jumbled pocket of boulders that looked like a good place for an ambush. Maybe he could hide there until he figured out how to rescue the girl.

It took him half an hour to reach the spot, for he took great care not to show himself. Once he had to dive flat to the ground behind a fallen yucca log as a pair of chattering boys went by, their bows in hand. They failed to see him, however, and Noel crept on, his heart pounding overtime.

He reached the rocks at last, eager to dig in, but just as he did so, an Apache warrior in a white man's shirt and a long breechclout rose from the rocks and trained an Army rifle on him.

The gun was battered and rusty. It probably hadn't been cleaned in years. But at this angle, the long bore of the muzzle was at Noel's eye level. It looked enormous, and lethal. He froze, the blood draining from his head in a rush that left him slightly dizzy. Slowly, he put up his hands.

The sentry shouted, and two other braves came running. One of them plucked the pistol from Noel's hand.

He looked into their dark, impassive faces. Their eyes held only hostility.

Noel knew better than to show any fear. He met their gazes as arrogantly as he could.

"I want to speak to Kansana," he said.

The braves grunted in scorn. The one holding the army rifle said in English, "You think you are clever, White Eyes.

But you do not escape us, no matter how many tricks you try. Take him back, Iotah, and tie him once again."

They lashed his hands behind his back. "Wait a minute," said Noel. "I'm not your prisoner. I'm—"

From the corner of his eye he saw the war club swinging through the air. He twisted on his heel in an effort to dodge it, but pain exploded through his skull and he fell into blackness.

CHAPTER 7

∞

The shock of water thrown in his face brought Noel abruptly awake. He groaned, rolling onto his side, and licked the water from his chapped lips. It tasted good. He longed for more.

A foot kicked him. He opened his eyes and sat up. He was kicked again, from all sides, until he got to his feet and stood swaying. He touched the throbbing spot on the back of his skull and winced.

He was surrounded by Apache braves, ranging from young boys to old men. Bronzed and lean, they stared at him with eyes like chipped flint. Their faces—flat-cheeked, strong-nosed, thin-lipped—gave nothing away. He was struck by a sense of an alien culture, an alien way of thought. He wondered if he would be able to communicate with them at all, not just with words but with meaning. He suspected they shared few points of reference.

"I've come in friendship—" he began, but one of them struck him.

"Do not speak."

Before he could protest, the circle parted to reveal a tall Apache with long gray hair falling to his shoulders. Squint lines around his deep-set eyes and grooves worn on either side of his wide, thin-lipped mouth spoke of his age. The Apache's bare chest was deep and powerfully muscled. A puckered white scar ran diagonally across his torso. Another scar ran the length of his left arm. His strong legs were crisscrossed with dozens of tiny scars.

His keen dark eyes commanded authority. At once Noel knew he was facing Kansana, leader of these people.

The Apache studied Noel in silence. Noel wanted to appeal to him, but he held his tongue as he'd been commanded.

At last, Kansana finished his inspection. Only then did his gaze shift beyond Noel. He pointed.

Noel turned around and saw Leon dangling against the cliff face, hanging by his arms. The sun was high overhead now, and its rays were just starting to strike Leon. He had been positioned to hang in the sun at the hottest time of the day.

Despite his dislike for his double, Noel could not ignore a swift prick of concern. Leon's eyes were shut. His face was bruised and skinned, puffy from too much sun exposure. Dried blood encrusted his lips. Shirtless and bootless, he hung motionless, not even moaning. Only the shallow rise and fall of his chest betrayed the fact that he still lived.

Noel didn't want to be near Leon at any time. He wished Leon didn't exist. But the senseless, sadistic brutality of this torture angered Noel. He turned back to Kansana with a hot glare.

Kansana held up two fingers. "Twins?" he said.

Stiffly Noel nodded.

"My youngest son Yotavo captured him," said Kansana with pride. "With only traditional Apache weapons, my son captured a White Eyes, his woman, and his horse. It was a good coup."

Noel considered saying something insulting, and thought better of it. Instead he said, "I have come to ransom the girl.

She is the granddaughter of Tom Trask."

Something flickered in Kansana's dark eyes. "Trask is known to us. He deals fairly with the *tinde*."

"He is very concerned about his granddaughter. He would like her back," said Noel.

"Why did Trask not come himself and ask?"

"He is old, and his son is dying," said Noel shortly. "El Raton's men burned his ranch."

Kansana nodded as though he knew this news already. Noel wondered how fast the Apache grapevine worked. Just how much could they communicate with steel mirrors? Or maybe someone hoofed it over the mountains every night with the midnight news report.

Noel waited, but Kansana wasn't much of a talker. Noel wished he hadn't gotten the bright idea to come here by himself. He suspected Don Emilio's smooth tongue would have been useful. Diplomacy wasn't Noel's strong suit.

He said, "Will you release her?"

"What does Trask offer?"

"What do you want?"

As soon as he spoke, Noel knew he'd said the wrong thing. Kansana's eyes narrowed. He turned away.

"Wait!" said Noel desperately. "Do you want cattle? Horses?"

Scorn rippled through the other braves. Tahzi, who had spoken to Noel last night, said, "Cattle we take. Horses we do not need."

Noel had already figured out his offer was pretty feeble. Cody had explained to him yesterday that an Apache could trot twenty miles in a day without tiring. If an Apache bothered to ride a horse, he was likely to eat it at the end of the day, aware that he could always steal another one.

"Guns," croaked a voice from behind him.

SHOWDOWN

Noel turned and saw Leon's swollen eyes cracked open. Although he was obviously in pain, Leon managed to glare his contempt at Noel.

"Give . . . guns," he gasped out.

Noel knew enough about old West history to recognize that as bad advice. Rifles would enable the Apaches to go on the warpath, killing ranchers and settlers in wholesale slaughter.

On the other hand, there was the girl, kneeling in the dirt and tied to a stake like a stray dog. Noel's eyes met her blue ones across the distance. She shook her head.

"Guns are good trade," said Kansana.

Noel hesitated, then shook his head. "I don't have any guns. Trask won't agree to that."

"Then there is no ransom."

"Kansana," said Noel sharply, "I have heard it said that you do not keep white captives—"

"My son will trade her to another band," said Kansana. "It is his right."

"I will trade you myself for her freedom," said Noel.

The Apaches conferred among themselves. Kansana listened to them. His face remained impassive; he said nothing.

At last he held up his hand to silence them. His gaze met Noel's. "You do not bargain for your brother."

"No," said Noel.

"White Eyes believe that the *tinde* are savages. They say we kill women and children, that we have no heart. I have strong sons. They are my pride; my heart runs with their swiftness."

Noel wasn't sure where Kansana was going. He waited, trying to curb his impatience.

"Tahzi left his lance in your camp last night. He says you ride with the grandson of Trask and a Mexican."

"Don Emilio Navarres," said Noel with a nod.

A murmur ran through the braves. Kansana smiled. "We steal much cattle from Don Emilio."

"Good going . . . Noel," croaked Leon hoarsely. "Come no plan . . . usual. You waiting for . . . rescue?"

"Shut up!" said Noel.

Leon laughed. It was a rasping husk of sound, broken off by a groan of misery.

Noel felt a shiver somewhere deep inside him. His duplicate was dying by slow, agonizing degrees.

"Trask has been fair with you," said Noel desperately. "Return that courtesy now by letting his granddaughter return to him."

Yotavo stepped forward with a swagger. He looked young and arrogant and dangerous. His black eyes gleamed with heat. "Let us see his big words when he is roasting over the slow fire. He seeks to trick us. The girl belongs to me. Why should I give her up for empty words?"

"Keeping peace with Trask is more important than your importance," said Tahzi sharply.

Yotavo scowled. "You are afraid to fight. You trust every White Eyes who speaks of peace. But there is no peace for our people. We have seen how they tricked the Tchiene. Now there are none of them. Soon there will be no Mescaleros or Chiricahuas."

"I had a long dream in the night," began an old man who was as skinny as a stick and so wrinkled and toothless he looked more like a mummy than a man.

But no one wanted to listen to his dream.

"Kansana," said Tahzi, "hear me. This one has Power. He is not like the other, who is weak. I saw him standing in strange light and he spoke Power words—"

"Perhaps it is Tahzi who had the dream," jeered Yotavo.

Some of the men chuckled. Tahzi's hand went to the long knife at his side, but Kansana held up his hand wearily.

SHOWDOWN

"Fighting among ourselves accomplishes nothing. If we keep the girl, Trask, Don Emilio, and all the other ranchers will band together to make war with us."

"They will send the soldiers—"

"Now Tahzi fears the soldiers," said Yotavo scornfully. "Tahzi fears the roadrunner. Tahzi fears his own shadow."

"Silence!" said Kansana sharply.

The youngsters obeyed, but Tahzi's eyes were drawn to smoldering slits and Yotavo smirked.

"Tahzi has wisdom, and you, Yotavo, see nothing but the end of your own war lance," said Kansana angrily. The smirk died from Yotavo's face. He glowered. "We have seen Victorio raise the warpath. He failed to drive away the White Eyes. Nana failed too. They put him in an iron cage and let all the White Eyes walk by to look at him. Now even Geronimo is defeated. Is this the shame we want?"

"If we do not fight, they will take all our land for theirs," said Yotavo.

"If we fight, they take it anyway," said Tahzi. "They are too many."

"Old woman," sneered Yotavo. "I do not fear them. Nana was old. Geronimo was old. Today I hear only the words of old men." His gaze, bold and hot, met Noel's. "Unless I have guns, many guns, I do not give back the girl."

Noel glared back, almost choking with frustration. Here stood Kansana, who was perfectly reasonable and willing to make a deal, and Yotavo just wanted to be bullheaded and cause more trouble.

"Told you," whispered Leon.

Noel ignored him. This mess was Leon's fault, and he was getting exactly what he deserved.

"Maybe Yotavo is afraid to be a man," said Noel, figuring he'd had enough of playing the cautious diplomat.

Yotavo grew still and intent, like a rattlesnake.

"A man, like Kansana, knows when to be merciful, when to make peace, and when to make war. A child makes many boasts, and is afraid to do what is wise."

The men chuckled. Beyond them, pretending to work hard at their tasks, even some of the women exchanged smiles.

Yotavo's face turned dark with rage. Whipping out his knife, he charged at Noel.

"Enough!" said Kansana sharply and gripped Yotavo's knife hand.

The boy strained a moment to get free, but although the cords in Kansana's neck stood out like ropes his strength was superior. The knife dropped in the dirt and glittered there like silver. Kansana released Yotavo, who stumbled back with a murderous glare.

Noel barely managed to hide his relief. It was about time old Kansana put loudmouth in his place. Now they'd get somewhere.

"There is much talk of manhood," said Kansana, and his voice was hard with anger. "Now we will have proof. You have offered yourself in exchange for the girl, White Eyes. We will take this offer."

The glow inside Noel faded. He met Kansana's gaze, and his whole being grew alert and careful. Without hesitation he nodded.

"There is more," said Kansana. "We will test you. If you prove yourself as much a man as an Apache, we will let you take the girl to her grandfather. Is it agreed?"

The braves murmured their approval. Tahzi looked worried, but he was nodding. Yotavo still glared in sullen rage.

"He will squirm for mercy like a maggot on a hot rock," said Yotavo with scorn. "Like the other one."

Noel noticed no one asked him if he went along with this twist in the deal. Apache torture wasn't something he wanted to experience. He didn't like the idea of trials of manhood either. These men had the advantage of being adapted to the climate and terrain. If they expected him to run a twenty-mile footrace, they could forget it.

"Why don't we compete with bows and arrows?" Noel asked. "Skill in marksmanship."

"Even a child can shoot the bow," said Yotavo.

Tahzi touched Noel's chest. "It is settled," he said. "Come."

"Wait a minute," said Noel in alarm, looking around and realizing the Apaches had scattered. "What's been settled? What are we going to do?"

Tahzi prodded him forward without answering. As Noel walked away, he heard Leon's rasping laugh.

Ten minutes later Noel found out what he had to do. At the mouth of the canyon, the cliff walls veered out and the ground was fairly level. In the past someone had built a corral across the mouth of the canyon, probably to trap wild horses or to pen cattle. Tall gateposts with a crosspiece overhead supported a dangling rope. The gate was long since gone, and most of the fence had fallen down, but the posts looked sturdy. Noel saw a handful of young warriors astride horses, milling in anticipation. The rest of the camp had gathered to watch, the women speaking sharply to children who wandered too close to the proceedings.

Yotavo rode the sorrel horse that had belonged to Leon. In his hands he was coiling a long bullwhip. Noel watched him a moment and felt suddenly icy cold despite the hundred-degree heat. He was beginning to suspect what they had in mind.

Kansana came up to him. "The men will take turns riding past you. Fifty strokes."

Noel blinked, and barely managed to hide his dismay. Pride demanded that he pull out his macho superman act, beat on his chest, and grunt expressively, but inside he wanted to be sick. He'd seen Roman floggings, with the victim's back shredded down to the bone and mangled flesh oozing blood. His breath left him, and he couldn't seem to get it back.

Kansana's eyes bored into him. "A man does not cry out in pain. Is this understood?"

Noel nodded.

"One cry, and you fail the test. The girl will stay and she will belong to Yotavo. If you remain silent, the girl will leave with you in safety."

Noel nodded again. Worried that his fear might show, he didn't want to look at Kansana. It took all the effort he possessed, but he managed to say breathlessly, "Deal."

Kansana nodded and walked away. The women were chattering and smiling coyly at the braves, who showed off fancy rider tricks for them. They galloped past with one hand brushing the ground or drove war lances into a small target painted on the gatepost or knelt on their mount's back to shoot arrows. The women fluttered, and the children whooped with admiration. In their midst, Lisa-Marie sat quietly, the rawhide noose still about her neck. Now and then one of the women jerked it, just to give her a reminder of what her place was.

When Noel walked by, he glanced at her. She was staring into the distance, her face pale but composed. Her blue eyes were blank as though trying to tune out what was happening.

He didn't blame her. He wasn't sure what he would feel in her place. But at the same time, he would have appreciated a look of gratitude. She didn't have to lead a pep rally for him, but a smile would be nice.

They stripped off his shirt and hung him upside down by his heels. At once the blood rushed to his head and started pounding in his ears. He swung gently in the hot wind, looking at the ground about three feet below him. The position made him feel vulnerable and helpless. He noticed that his back was to the starting point of the riders. That meant he couldn't see them coming, would have only his hearing to warn him.

He heard hoofbeats approaching like thunder. Closing his eyes, Noel steeled himself as best he could. He heard the faint whistle of leather flying through air, then fire exploded in him with such force he felt cut in half. His eyes flew open and he fought for breath, too stunned to do more than dimly register a blurred shape of horse and rider galloping past him.

The rider wheeled and looped back, handing the whip to the next brave. The hoofbeats came at Noel again. The fire across his chest and back was spreading, like acid burning through his skin. Then the second lash wrapped around him, crossing the first one. He jerked and barely held back a grunt of agony.

By the time ten strokes had been delivered, he was blind and shuddering, barely able to keep from screaming for them to stop. He didn't think he could last through five more, much less the whole fifty. The pain was beyond comprehension, countless layers of it overlapping his consciousness. Some of the riders were better at wielding the whip than others. Some of the blows came clumsily; others bit into him like razor wire. He was spun around and around by the impetus of the lashes. Some caught him on the chest, some on the side, some across the back, some all the way around. He could feel his blood dripping hot on his skin. He saw splatters of it being absorbed by the dust below him.

Yet the lashes kept coming. Time after time he felt himself skidding toward the blessed relief of unconsciousness, yet each blow brought him back to full awareness. It grew harder and harder to hold back his cries of pain. He could feel each scream hit against his clenched teeth, and it took all his will, all his strength, to remain silent.

No matter how hard they hit him, he refused to be beaten. He learned to expel his breath just before the blow so that he had no air to make an outcry. Sweaty blood dripped into his eyes, salty and stinging. He blinked fiercely, finding his whole consciousness focused down to this battle of wills, this determination not to surrender.

The next lash caught him across the stomach, low, right along the edge of his trousers. Bile hit the back of his throat, and he almost choked on it. When it was gone, he gasped for air, miserable with the sourness of it lingering in his throat and nostrils.

His thoughts wandered, and he remembered when he was a child learning how to dive. He must have been five or six years old, a skinny, shivering boy crouched on the edge of the lap pool built in the basement of their home. The concrete dug into his knees. Chlorine reeked in the damp, stuffy air. Artificial lights hung from the low ceiling, and the water looked black and oily. At night it haunted his nightmares. He called it the lagoon of the monster. He knew that eventually the monster would rise from the murky depths of the pool and come upstairs to drag him from his bed down to the basement. It would stash him at the bottom of the pool the way crocodiles stashed meat to rot it before eating. His parents would search for him, but they would never find him at the black bottom of the pool, not until it was drained for cleaning. Now his father expected, no, demanded, him to dive into the water headfirst, straight into the jaws waiting beneath the surface.

The monster didn't eat his father because his father didn't believe in it. But Noel believed. He could see its yellow eyes glowing at him from the depths, and nothing could have convinced him that it was only the reflection of the overhead lights.

"Jump, Noel, dammit!" said his father. "Duck your head and go right in. I'll catch you."

Gasping with terror, Noel hesitated between the death he expected and his father's wrath.

"Noel!"

He launched himself at the water, and it closed over him like death.

"Forty-four," said Kansana's voice, steady and without inflection.

Noel surfaced dimly into the brightness and heat. The wet saltiness he smelled was blood, not chlorine. He had almost drowned before his father lifted him from the pool. Noel dragged in a lungful of hot desert air and remembered his father's warm breath blown into his mouth. His father had been crying. He'd cracked one of Noel's ribs while trying to pound the water out. Later, wrapped in a blanket, Noel had been held in his father's arms upstairs in bed until he fell asleep. When he woke up the next morning, he saw his father's beard-stubbled face on the pillow and his father's large hand was still clasped around Noel's.

"Forty-five."

Noel wanted his father now, wanted him with an intensity that *hurt.* His father had been a mathematician. Everything existed in black and white absolutes for him. He did not see the gray shading of human interpersonal dynamics the way Noel did. What happened in history did not interest him. It was the here and now that mattered to Jeffrey Kedran. Time travel intrigued him only because of the mathematical theories involved. Building a time computer fascinated him; using one never tempted him at all.

"Forty-nine."

Yotavo must have taken the last turn. Noel heard the horse coming faster than any had before. The sound of the whip in the air was shrill, vicious. The pop of leather and the rip of flesh came simultaneously. Noel felt something give within himself, as though his will had broken. He felt the scream tear itself out from the depths of him and go hurtling out.

His mouth opened. He gasped for air, but no sound came. He fainted first.

CHAPTER 8

∞

"Cut him down," said a harsh voice.

He was only a faint pinprick of consciousness. The blazing sun had burned away the rest of him. Every thought was feeble, a dim flicker of awareness that came and went.

The taut rawhide cords twanged beneath the strike of a knife. Leon fell in a heap on the ground, his shoulders screaming with raw agony. He was kicked over onto his side. The knife cut through the bonds on his wrists, and his arms fell free of each other. He groaned.

"Tend him," said the same harsh voice.

Leon faded, but the wet coolness of water upon his face brought him back. He blinked and squinted, forcing open his swollen eyes.

His vision was blurred, and at first he could see nothing. The terrible heat was gone, however. They had dragged him into the shade. He drew in a cool breath, and felt life returning by slow degrees.

More water upon his face . . . cool wetness upon his lips. He drank in sudden, choking eagerness, reaching blindly for the gourd dipper, causing the water to spill.

"Careful," said Lisa-Marie's voice.

He drank more, and the dry ache in his throat eased. A sigh of relief escaped him. He licked his cracked, swollen lips and tried to focus on her.

His vision was still blurred, but improving. Her oval face swam before him. He saw the tangled spill of her hair, the thick curls glinting a dozen shades of gold, platinum, wheat, honey, and auburn. Burnished, beautiful hair... an abundance cascading upon her shoulders. In longing, he reached up one of his numb hands and tried to touch one of her curls.

She jerked back. "Don't touch me," she snapped.

Her voice was rough with hostility and something else. Her eyes looked red and puffy. Had she been crying?

He closed his eyes and gathered enough strength to reach into her mind. Swirling confusion, anger like a crimson bath, fear lancing here and there with icicles of clarity. He found memory, and a floodgate opened, showing him a dusty scene of a man trussed by the heels, hanging upside down like a slab of beef, and the Apache riders hurtling at this target...

Leon felt the sting of the lash, and jerked.

But it wasn't happening now. It had already taken place while he was semiconscious, dying in the sun. Amazement trickled through Leon. Before, when they were in medieval Greece together, his attempt to have Noel murdered had backfired because whatever pain Noel felt Leon felt too. Now either his own debilitation was blocking the link to Noel, or the link was fading.

Am I becoming real?

Hope filled him. Leon pushed himself to one elbow.

"Where... is he?" he whispered hoarsely.

Lisa-Marie had seated herself on a rock away from him, but at his question she glanced his way. Tear tracks streaked her dirty cheeks. She did not answer.

Leon sat up, although the world spun around him. "Where is he? Is he dead?"

Wide-eyed, still crying, she pressed her hand to her lips and swiftly shook her head.

The young Apache called Tahzi appeared. A squaw in a shapeless deerskin dress followed him. She carried Leon's hat and a canteen. At Tahzi's gesture, she laid these items on the ground beside Leon.

"You go," said Tahzi in slurred English.

Leon squinted at the sky beyond the shaggy top of the salt cedar tree casting shade over him. The sun was still high. "Now?" he said.

Tahzi frowned and pointed emphatically at the end of the canyon. "You go now," he said.

Lisa-Marie rose to her feet. She stood waiting for Leon with her back to him. She made no effort to help him as he staggered and struggled to his feet. The circulation was returning to his hands, bringing new agony. He found it difficult to grasp his hat brim and finally crammed the hat on his head with the heels of his hands. Getting the canteen strap slung over his shoulder was even harder. When he finally stood erect, he had to close his eyes against an attack of vertigo. He felt hot from sunburn and his thoughts were scrambled. It was hard to remember what he was supposed to do.

Lisa-Marie followed Tahzi and the squaw. Leon stumbled after her. When he left the shade and emerged into the blazing heat once again, he flinched and cringed, holding up a hand to shield his watering eyes.

The children—skinny, beady-eyed creatures—buzzed around him like mosquitoes, jeering and slapping him from all sides. He did his best to ignore them, although their scorn infuriated him.

"Cries hard," they chanted, skipping alongside. "Cries-Like-Baby!"

Some of the women smiled as he stumbled past them. Hard smiles of superiority, faint and mocking. He flushed. So what if he'd groveled for mercy when they'd been torturing him? What was he supposed to do? Take it in silence?

Leon believed in making any deal at any time in order to survive. Even now, it looked like the Apaches were letting him and the girl go. Noel must have passed the test, but where was he?

Ahead stood a small cluster of braves, waiting near the mouth of the canyon. The women began to run about, snatching up possessions and packing baskets. His hopes sank. Maybe the Indians weren't letting them go. Maybe they were just breaking camp.

Lisa-Marie halted about twenty feet short of the men waiting near the tall gateposts. Leon limped up beside her and stopped too. He felt short of breath and exhausted as though he'd walked miles instead of a few yards. Two braves still sat on their ponies. With a cold feeling low in his gut, Leon noticed one of the riders was Yotavo, who had captured him in the first place.

Maybe this was just another Apache game. He hated all of them.

Kansana, tall with gray hair and terrible scars, stepped forward. His eyes swept coldly over Leon. "Your brother has done well," he said. "He has great courage. Alone he came here to give ransom. With his courage he bought the life of this woman. You, Cries-Like-Baby, we give to him also, although he did not ask for your life."

Leon flushed with anger. His gaze sought out Noel, who was standing among the men. The old rivalry and hatred swept through Leon like a grass fire. What gave Noel the right to decide he was something worthless to be discarded?

You didn't get rid of me this time, thought Leon. *You will never get rid of me.*

Kansana walked away. Tahzi pointed at the mouth of the canyon. "Go," he said.

The other braves melted away, leaving Noel standing alone. Glaring at him, Leon noticed that Noel was oddly stiff and drawn as though his clothing hurt him. His face might have been carved from stone, and only its pallor gave him away. Then his gray eyes lifted to meet Leon's.

Across that short distance something leapt between them and connected. Noel's pain lanced into Leon, who staggered and nearly fell down. Leon gripped Lisa-Marie's arm to steady himself, and fought to break the link with Noel for his own self-preservation.

It would not snap, but finally he succeeded in muting it. His old fear surfaced. If something happened to Noel, Leon did not think he could survive it.

Angrily he turned and called after the Apaches, "Kansana! Tahzi! Give us horses at least."

Only Tahzi glanced back. He scowled. "You have lives. Is enough."

"My brother will die if he has to walk all the way back—"

"His spirit is strong," said Tahzi with a swift glance of respect at Noel. "He will not die."

"Wait!"

But Tahzi was gone. Only Yotavo and the other brave waited on their horses. Yotavo's black eyes smoldered with resentment. He pointed, and Leon started walking. Lisa-Marie kept step in silence.

When they drew even with Noel, he fell in with them. Leon did not like being this close to his double. It was like standing next to a powerful energy generator and feeling the current oscillate into your own electrical system. The friction scratching between their bodies sang on Leon's nerves.

Noel moved slowly like an old man. Smears of blood had dried on his face and neck. Fresh blood seeped through his plaid shirt in places where the cloth stretched tight against his side. His gaze was focused inward, and his lean, chiseled face remained impassive.

Beyond the clearing, the trail grew narrow and rough. It was necessary to crouch down and jump into a shallow crevice, then scramble over a series of boulders to where the trail resumed.

At this point Yotavo and his companion reined up. Leon's back itched with vulnerability. He wondered if Yotavo would plant an arrow in them, but none came.

When he glanced back a few seconds later, Yotavo and the other man were gone.

Lisa-Marie jumped first into the crevice. Leon and Noel looked at each other. Leon gestured irritably for Noel to go next.

Noel crouched slowly, as though he might shatter if he bent his body. When he jumped, he grunted with pain and nearly fell.

Only Lisa-Marie's grab of his arm kept him on his feet. He staggered to a rock and leaned there, gasping and white-faced. Leon had his own problems getting down. The pain in his swollen hands was almost unbearable, and the deep cuts in his wrists throbbed. He found it agonizing to lift his arms even a few inches.

Even so, he didn't feel as bad as Noel looked. He stared at his double critically.

"Can you make it?" he asked. "The trail will be rough all the way down the mountain—"

"Yeah," said Noel, choking out the word.

"He can barely walk," said Lisa-Marie. "The heat will—"

"Go," said Noel. Through half-shut lids, his eyes shimmered as though they were melting. He pushed himself away from the rock's support and walked on like an automaton.

Leon had no sense of time. It seemed an eternity before

they reached the foot of the mountain. The heat increased until it seemed they were descending into an inferno. He tried to keep his face shaded with his hat brim, but everywhere the sun touched him felt as though he were being fried in oil. He wasn't always certain if the water on his face was perspiration or tears. Noel's silence chafed him. How could Noel be so much stronger? How could he endure the torment he was suffering without a word, without a moan? How could he keep walking when he must be ready to collapse?

At the bottom of the mountain, they paused to rest in the scant shade of a dead tree. A hawk was nesting in the top branches. It flew, its cry a thin scree on the hot wind.

To the west, the sun sank low. They had perhaps a couple of hours yet before nightfall.

Leon wiped his face. "We'd better wait till the sun goes down before we go on," he said.

As he spoke he glanced involuntarily at Noel, who was sitting cross-legged on the ground with his back ramrod stiff. Noel opened his eyes and gave Leon a brief nod.

"Pass around the canteen," said Lisa-Marie. Her bare arms were pink with sunburn, and she had been limping a long while. "I'm so hot I could smother."

Leon did not move. "Do you know where the next water hole is?"

"No."

He sighed. "Then we'd better wait till later to have a drink."

She glared at him but didn't argue. Instead she touched Noel's arm with a gentle hand. He flinched, and she flinched too.

"I'm sorry!" she cried. "Can't we do anything for you?"

Jealousy burned in Leon. He was hurt also, yet Lisa-Marie spared no sympathy for him.

"Nothing," said Noel tightly as though even speaking hurt. "I'm fine." He turned his head and met Leon's furious gaze. A flicker of a smile touched his lips. "Allies for once. Weird for us, isn't it?"

Leon stared at him, too astonished to answer.

"You're in charge," said Noel. He shifted position and winced. "You get us home."

The sun crept lower, and the hot wind blew incessantly, swaying the weeds. Before them the world was infinity, empty miles stretching in all directions. Yet the emptiness was an illusion, just as the vision of water shimmering a few hundred yards away was not real. Somewhere in this wasteland were people, shelter, water, and food. Leon could not remember the direction they were supposed to go.

While he struggled with himself, debating on whether to betray his incompetence by asking, Noel stretched out on the hot ground and lay there like a dead man, hatless and diminished in the sunshine. Grasshoppers as brown as toast whirred by, jumping in search of food. A jackrabbit ambled near them, then froze, its long ears pink beneath the brown fur. If Leon squinted his eyes just so, he could envision Noel as a skeleton lying there, white bones bleached in the sun and picked clean by beetles.

The image frightened him more than he wanted to admit.

He poked his own throbbing palm, taking pleasure in the pain he dealt himself, as though to confirm his own existence. He knew he was less than whole. Something crucial in him had always been missing.

He was a blurred, imperfect copy. Shorter than Noel by nearly an inch, his skin was pitted, his jaw not as lean. His features were less chiseled. His eyes held less gray, less color. He could eat but not taste the food. He could look at Lisa-Marie's beauty and long to possess her, yet passion was a shadow to him. He could pretend that he was not different, yet the truth always lay in him deep.

"We won't have to walk the whole way," said Lisa-Marie.

Her voice startled Leon from his thoughts. He lifted his hot face from where it had been resting on his knees. "What?"

"I said we won't have to walk the whole way. My grandfather and brother will be looking for us." She paused a moment, then looked straight at Leon. "When they find us, they'll string you up from a cottonwood tree and let the buzzards pick you clean."

"That's not—"

"—*fair*?" she finished for him. Her blue eyes flashed with scorn. "And just what do you think you deserve? You burned our ranch. You tried to kill my family. You carried me off like a sack of potatoes—"

"I *care* about you," he said desperately. "I just wanted to get to know—"

"Don't insult me like that!" she retorted, scarlet-cheeked. "You're nothing but a bandit. If I had a gun right now I'd shoot you myself."

His eyes narrowed, and he felt ugliness replace his admiration for her. "Watch what you say. Right now you need me."

"For protection?" She laughed with scorn. "You're useless with Apaches. It took your brother to get us free. If it weren't for him we'd still be prisoners back there, and—"

"I would have gotten us free!" said Leon. "I just needed time."

"Don't lie to yourself, mister. You ought to be thanking your brother instead of—"

"I'll go to hell before I thank him for anything!"

"I think we're already there," said Noel softly, startling them both.

At once Lisa-Marie knelt beside him. "Do you want some water? You, help him sit up."

Leon felt the urge to hurl the canteen into the brush. Instead, he gripped Noel by the arms and pulled him upright. Noel shuddered in his grasp, sending his pain into Leon, and Leon released him swiftly to avoid more agony.

Noel swayed and would have toppled over had Lisa-Marie not steadied him.

"You fool!" she said to Leon. "Be careful with him."

"My name is Leon, not hey-you," he retorted.

"I know that," she said, undaunted. "Give him some water. Please."

Noel was staring dreamily at the sunset. He roused though at the taste of water and gulped it eagerly until Leon took the canteen away.

Lisa-Marie wiped the mouth of the canteen and limited herself to small, careful sips. Then it was Leon's turn. He drank, feeling the coolness but not the taste, and hated both of the others for what they had.

"I'll carry it," said Lisa-Marie. "You help him up."

Leon wanted to argue, but he recognized the futility of that. Handing over the canteen, he pulled Noel to his feet. Noel's skin was burning hot, even through the cloth of his shirt. His eyes were so dilated, they looked black. For a moment he stared deep into Leon's eyes.

Feeling vulnerable and exposed in that scrutiny, Leon shuddered. He stepped away quickly, but Noel sagged and would have fallen had Leon not caught him.

For a moment they clung together, and Leon felt something akin to pity stir within him. He thrust that emotion away, reminding himself that Noel had all the advantages. Noel didn't need pity. He needed taking down a peg.

But Leon didn't release his grip on his double. Putting his arm around Noel, he steadied him. With a muted groan, Noel managed to straighten at last. He set his teeth, biting off a gasp.

Touching this way, it was almost impossible to mute the empathic link between them. Leon felt fresh sweat break out across his forehead. He couldn't maintain this physical contact much longer.

Perhaps Noel sensed this, for he pulled away. "I'm fine now," he said, still gritting his teeth. "Thanks."

Relieved, Leon released him. He knew Noel was lying, but it didn't matter.

"Still trying to prove you're better than everyone else?" he murmured savagely. "Still showing off for the girl?"

Noel ignored him. They started walking, their pace so slow it would take them weeks to finish the journey before them. Noel seemed to be concentrating solely on placing his feet and keeping his balance, but he said, "Did the Indian who captured you—"

"Yotavo."

"Did Yotavo knock you out when he first caught you?"

"Yes," said Leon in surprise. "How did you—did you feel it?"

"Yes."

"But the link doesn't work both ways!" said Leon before he realized he was giving too much away.

A ghost of a smile played upon Noel's clamped lips. "Not usually, no. For a moment I thought you were dead."

"You won't get rid of me that easily."

"No."

Leon wrestled a moment with his own stubborn pride, but his curiosity was too strong. "What happened to us? I thought you were going back to—uh—back to—"

"Chicago," said Noel with a warning glance at Lisa-Marie's back that Leon didn't need.

"Yeah. You promised to leave me where I was. Damn you, why didn't you do it?"

"I didn't have any choice. I warned you there was a

seventy-eight percent chance that you would be brought through with me."

Leon grunted. He had no interest in percentages. "So why here?"

"It wasn't my idea," said Noel sharply. "The saboteur closed the time loop. We can't get back."

Leon started laughing. The sound rolled across the plain and echoed off the ridges behind them.

"It's not funny," said Noel. "You—" He winced and pressed a hand to his side, shutting his eyes a moment.

Leon went on chuckling. "I think it's marvelous. Just think, for the rest of eternity you're trapped. And wherever you go, there I'll be. A perpetual thorn in your side. Believe me, I intend to cause trouble everywhere I go, just for the joy of watching you try to clean it up."

"We could work together," said Noel. "Try to pool our resources and get back. We don't have to be enemies."

"Why shouldn't we be enemies?" asked Leon furiously. "Every second of your existence reminds me of what I'm not, of what I can't have."

Noel scowled. "Are you going to whine about that forever? You exist, don't you?"

"Finally you admit it!"

"I've never denied you. How could I?"

"You'd like to," accused Leon.

Noel stopped. "Sure I would. You shouldn't be here. You cause trouble at every chance. This mess, for instance. None of it would have happened if you hadn't interfered."

"I didn't urge El Raton to attack Trask's ranch."

"No, but you helped, didn't you? And you kidnapped Lisa-Marie."

Leon tucked in his chin, his mouth clamping down tight with resentment. "She's pretty," he muttered.

"Is that license to grab her?"

"Shut up," said Leon.

Ahead of them, walking along in her squaw dress and moccasins, Lisa-Marie had to be hearing every word, but she never glanced back. He could feel her listening, however. He could feel the anger and resentment building inside her like an imminent explosion. Every word Noel said just made it worse.

Leon snaked his head around at Noel and said, "Just shut up."

"Why didn't you hypnotize those Apaches and get yourself out?" muttered Noel. "Why didn't you rescue yourself?"

If his hands hadn't been so stiff and painful, Leon would have curled them into fists and pummeled Noel. Rage seethed in his throat like scalding acid. He glared, but said nothing. He wasn't about to let Noel know that his powers didn't always work.

"Feeling sorry for yourself?" he said finally to Noel. "She thinks you're some kind of hero now. If you expect me to be grateful, don't waste your time."

Noel's thin nostrils flared. His face looked ghostly in the lavender hue of twilight. Ahead, the sky blazed with magnificent jewel tones of color. The wind had ceased, and the air felt cool and hushed. *False peace,* thought Leon. *Death waits for the weak here at every turn.*

"You," said Noel hoarsely, "can't exist without me. You *need* me. But I don't need you in return. Remember that when the time comes."

"What time?" said Leon irritably. "What kind of threat is that?"

But Noel didn't answer.

CHAPTER 9

∞

Less than an hour later, as they were trudging along the sandy bottom of a draw, Noel made a faint sound and collapsed in a heap. He did it so quietly that at first Leon thought he had sunk down to rest.

But when Leon turned back and set a hand on Noel's shoulder, he could not rouse him. The fever in his double rushed across that bridge of physical contact, filling Leon with sweating torment.

With a gasp, he jerked his hand away and knelt in the sand, shuddering in an effort to clear Noel's pain from his system. The link, however, was always there, no matter how much he tried to shake it. Feeling clammy and ill, Leon stared at the dark shape of his twin.

"You need me," Noel had just said. "You can't exist without me."

It was true. No matter how much Leon tried to deny it, he knew it was true.

Lisa-Marie turned back to join them. She knelt on the other side of Noel with a sigh. "I'm surprised he went this far," she said.

Her voice reminded him of a muffled bell. She was holding herself back, making her tone flat and disinterested, in an effort at self-protection, but now and then the rich, melodious timbre of her voice came through. Leon shivered.

He looked at her, hair glinting pale in the moonlight's cold sheen, the rest of her in shadow. To him, she was a crystal holding all the reflected beauty of starlight. The tough fiber of her mind and the fierceness of her emotions—made even stronger for being held in check—combined like a volcanic force beneath an outward grace and beauty as delicate as porcelain.

He ached to tell her what he felt, but he dared not make himself more vulnerable to her contempt.

Instead, he curled his hands into fists and pressed his knuckles deep into the sand while she bent over Noel. He could touch the edges of her mind as he dared not touch her body. He sensed the concern flow from her to his double. Jealousy burned at his core.

"Leave him be," he said. "We have to keep going."

"Aren't you going to help him?" she asked. "We can't just let him lie here."

"If he can't keep up, we'll have to leave him behind."

"No!" she cried sharply. "You ungrateful good-for-nothing! He saved your life."

"And now he could put us at risk again," said Leon. "We have to keep going. We're not safe yet."

"The Apaches let us go. Kansana won't go back on his word."

"He might."

"Apaches are honest," she said in exasperation. "Unlike some people I could name, they never lie."

Leon snorted. "Everyone lies."

"How stupid you are! Are you going to argue with me forever? Make a camp. Find some sort of shelter. Hunt us something to eat. He's burning with fever. He needs to be kept warm. At least build a fire."

Leon got to his feet. "I'm not your slave."

She also stood, facing him with her hands on her hips. "No, but he is your brother. You owe him—"

"I owe him nothing!"

"Just your life!" she retorted. "Or would you rather be still hanging by your thumbs in that canyon? Are you dead to all decency? Have you no conscience left, no shred of—"

He gripped her wrist and yanked her close. "You think he's a hero. Let me tell you this: He's *nothing*! All he does is meddle and interfere—"

"In this case I'm glad he did," she said, breathless but still defiant.

He could hear her heartbeat thudding fast. He could feel the hot shift of her thoughts as she desperately tried to think of a way to escape him. His grip dug deeper into her flesh, crushing her, hurting her to make her fear him.

"I saw you first," he said in a low, guttural voice.

She shoved at him with her free hand. "Get away from me!"

He laughed, feeding on her fury and fear, and twisted his fingers in her hair with a harshness that made her cry out. He kissed her, but her lips were wood and gave him nothing.

Her humiliation and disgust flooded his senses so overwhelmingly he released her. She staggered off balance and fell to her knees. Leon touched his mouth, raging that there was nothing for him in that caress. Why was he sentenced forever to be this half creature, this ghost who was real enough for others to see and touch yet was incomplete inside? Why could he only taste and feel and crave through the emotions of others? Why was there only hatred in him, when he wanted so much to love her and be loved?

Noel stirred and tried to push himself upright. "Leon, no," he gasped.

"Shut up. You're weak. You're worthless."

Lisa-Marie crawled between them. "No, *you're* the one who is worthless," she said. "He saved us, and you would have gotten us killed."

Leon bent toward her and hissed. She retaliated by throwing a fistful of sand in his face.

"Get out of here! Go on! We'll make do without you. Tuck your yellow tail between your legs and run."

"We'll stick together," said Noel. His voice was like a thread, yet it held enough determination to make both Leon and Lisa-Marie look at him. "Don Emilio and Cody are nearby. Should be. Find them. We'll be safe."

"Cody?" she said with a gasp and pressed her hands to her face. She was crying now. "Cody's alive?"

Noel reached his hand out to Leon. "Help me . . . up."

Leon hesitated a moment, then the temptations to desert them both faded within him. He gripped Noel's hand in his, his own flesh shrinking from physical contact with his twin, and dragged Noel upright. He tucked his shoulder under Noel's arm, and heard Noel's sharp intake of breath.

"Walk, damn you," muttered Leon.

Together they staggered down the draw. Noel took a few steps, then sagged again. Feeling the sick ebb of energy within his own limbs, Leon cursed Noel for doing this to him. If Noel would only try, they could probably break the link. But Noel was as stubborn as he was stupid.

You can't exist without me.

The threat reverberated in Leon's head, making it throb. Still manhandling Noel's limp weight, he reached a spot where the bank rose at a steep angle. Its base had been cut away by erosion, making a slight overhang. Panting, Leon eased Noel to the ground and rested a moment before dragging him under the scant shelter.

Lisa-Marie had fallen behind. Leon glanced around wildly in the darkness, afraid he'd lost her. Then she appeared, a blurred shadow in the darkness, and kicked two dried tumbleweeds against his feet.

"These will help get a fire started," she said. She dropped the scant collection of twigs and twisted mesquite roots that she'd gathered. "If you can find some dried cow patties, they burn the best."

Eventually they collected enough fuel to make a meager fire inside a ring of stones. It was a fitful, smoky little blaze, but it created an illusion of warmth against the dropping desert temperature. It also cast a small circle of light, making the darkness a wall surrounding them. He felt as though he sat inside a room with her.

Across the fire, with her tangled hair hanging over her shoulder and dirt streaked across her face, she was more beautiful than ever. She unscrewed the top from the canteen and allowed herself a few careful sips, then passed it to him.

He gulped recklessly to assuage his thirst, until she jerked it away.

"That's enough," she said angrily. "This one canteen has to last for days maybe. I don't know where the water holes are anymore. We have to ration this carefully."

Leon said nothing, just licked the few remaining drops of moisture from his chapped lips. Maybe distance would break the link and free him from Noel. He didn't think Noel was going to die from a whipping. Not really die. Leon thought about controlling Lisa-Marie's mind and making her go with him, leaving Noel behind.

But in Greece, when he had touched a vibrant young girl's mind and put her under his control it had changed her. She had lost the spark that made her so vital, and she had not regained it.

SHOWDOWN

He hesitated now to do the same thing to Lisa-Marie. Even if she went on scorning him, it was better than seeing her turn into a soulless husk.

Noel moaned and tried to move. At once Lisa-Marie flew to his side and quieted him.

"He's bled through his shirt. We should get it off and wash these cuts before they become infected."

Leon did not move from his place by the fire. "You just said we had to conserve our water. Leave him be."

"Bring the canteen here."

He met her imperious eyes and shook his head.

"Don't be stupid!" she snapped. "He has fever. He needs a drink."

Leon met her eyes a moment longer, then looked away and refused to move.

She huffed past him, snatched the canteen off the ground with such force he could hear the water sloshing inside it, and returned to Noel. With soft murmurs of encouragement she coaxed Noel to drink, and Leon closed his eyes as he felt the relief go through his twin.

Leon drew up his knees and rested his face on them. He did not look up until Lisa-Marie came back to the dying fire.

She stared at him a long while. "Don't you care?" she finally asked. "He's your brother, your *twin*. Now he's hurt bad and you don't even want to help him. Why do you hate him so much?"

"You wouldn't understand."

"I have a twin brother," she said proudly. "Sometimes it used to be almost like we could tell what the other one was thinking. He's like my own heartbeat, even though we've been apart for years. I couldn't just turn my back on him if he was hurt and needed me."

"You need me," Noel had said. Leon looked down at his clenched fists. Why had Noel taunted him like that?

"I guess you're just rotten all the way through," said Lisa-Marie. "I'm going to get some sleep. You keep watch. And don't you come near me, you hear?"

Her words sent his rage boiling over the top. Glaring at her, Leon hit her hard with his mind, using a single punch of mental force. Her eyes lost focus and rolled up, then she crumpled.

He let her lie on the ground in a heap. He glared at her a long while, breathing hard, his hands clenching and unclenching. She had no right to accuse him. She had no right to distrust him. He'd never done anything to her until now. But when she woke up, she'd think twice before she insulted him again.

The loneliness of the night closed around him like a fist. He let the fire die and shivered there, hugging himself with his sore arms. Beyond the chirping song of crickets, coyotes howled. Overhead a hawk sailed in silhouette across the moon.

He sensed only Noel and Lisa-Marie near him. Nothing else. And the emptiness inside him grew into a yawning chasm of black loneliness. He realized he needed people around him, hordes of people. He needed towns. He needed life. Out here, in the vast empty reaches of the desert, he had only himself. Without other life forces overlapping his, he could see too clearly the shadowy thinness of his own essence.

You need me . . .

He clapped his hands over his ears, but the words lingered in his mind.

He was a freak, an anomaly. He wasn't supposed to exist. His creation had been an accident in a warped time stream.

Well, accident or not, he did exist and he wasn't giving that up.

The moon was going down. The breeze died, and the

earth held its breath. He could feel prickles along his spine, primitive reactions on an instinctual, subconscious level to the darkness, to the night, to this savage land.

For a moment he toyed with the temptation to steal the canteen and walk away into the night.

But where would he go? He did not want to stay in this era. He did not want to stay in this horrible country.

Most of all, he feared that if he cut himself off from these two people and struck out alone, he would cease to exist. Each passing second seemed to diminish him. He imagined that if he lifted his hand now, he would be able to see right through it.

A jolt of alarm pulled his wits together. He raised his head, aware of something different. Something was happening, not just to him but to . . . *Noel.*

He was losing his twin. The link was fading.

Exhilaration blossomed inside him, only to be crushed by fear. He scrambled away from the cold ashes of the fire and found his twin huddled on the ground, shivering and tossing, his skin burning hot.

"Noel," he whispered, and put his hand on Noel's shoulder.

Noel flinched, and Leon felt the pain caused by his own touch. He took his hand away.

"Tell me how to help you. Noel? Listen to me. Can't you use emergency recall? Pull us out of this place, and that will heal you."

Another spasm went through Noel. He gripped Leon's leg, and only then did Leon realize he was conscious. Fear rippled through Leon. He hadn't sensed it. He hadn't *known.*

"I'm fading," Leon whispered urgently, gripping Noel's hand. "I am losing you. Don't leave me here. Damn you, Noel—"

"LOC," said Noel, gasping out the word as though it was to be his last. *"LOC!"*

"It doesn't work for me. You know that."

Noel made no answer. Leon ran his fingers over Noel's hot face. He had slipped from consciousness again. Leon felt a coldness inside that was colder than the limbo of the time stream.

Desperately he clawed the silver cuff from Noel's wrist. He pressed the hidden controls. He spoke urgently to the computer again and again, but it refused to activate for him.

It shouldn't be able to tell the difference. Weren't they duplicates? Its isomorphics weren't that sophisticated.

But it hadn't worked for him when he stole it from Noel in Greece, and it wouldn't work for him now.

The coldness inside him was increasing to the point of painfulness. Leon dropped the LOC, and when he tried to pick it up his fingers almost passed through it.

"Concentrate," he told himself.

Holding himself together took all the willpower he possessed. Panic nibbled at the edges of his mind until he wanted to scream. Before, when he'd ordered an assassination attempt on Noel, he had shared Noel's pain but he hadn't faded like this.

But there were other people before, he reminded himself. There was a whole medieval town to draw life essence and support from. Until now, he hadn't realized he received his own energy from others, drawing strength from the radiant glow of the life forces around him. He could not exist alone.

"Noel," he whispered urgently. "Tell me what to do. Wake up and activate the LOC."

Noel did not stir. By concentrating so hard he shook, Leon was able to hold himself together enough to pick up the LOC and place it back on Noel's wrist. Then he took Noel's other hand and pressed it over the LOC. He took Noel's forefinger and used it to push the control button.

The LOC hummed momentarily, then stopped.

Leon could have shouted with frustration. He shook Noel. "Wake up! You must wake up."

Noel remained slack in his hands, unconscious, unhelpful.

Snarling to himself, Leon smacked his palm against Noel's chest, feeling the stickiness of blood where the shirt cloth was glued to Noel's skin. Noel arched his back in agony and gave a shuddering moan.

Leon gripped him by the shoulder and half pulled him up. "Activate the LOC. Noel, activate the LOC!"

From the corner of his eye he was aware of Lisa-Marie waking up and coming to them. "What are you doing to him?" she demanded. "Leave him alone!"

Leon ignored her. "Noel! You can hear me. You know what is happening. Don't let it. Activate the LOC! Now!"

Noel's gray eyes opened, but would not focus. He mumbled something unintelligible. Leon cupped the back of Noel's head in his palm. He bent Noel's head toward him.

"Listen to me! You must—"

His hands ceased to be tangible. Noel slipped right through his grasp and thudded to the ground. Leon reached for him, but he could no longer grip anything solid. He screamed, but there was no sound.

Desperate, panic-stricken, he sent his mind hurtling at Noel's. He knew Noel's mind was impervious to his own, but it was all he had left.

Noel, he screamed silently. *Noel, help me! I need you!*

The coldness permeated his bones like ice. He looked down at himself and could see himself spreading so thin he was dissolving into the air. Other objects were visible through his body. It was as though the time vortex had opened and was drawing him into it.

Perhaps, he thought in hope, the emergency recall was working at last. If the dolts in the twenty-sixth century had finally fixed their malfunctioning equipment, perhaps he and Noel were going home at last to their proper time.

He looked at Noel, but his twin wasn't moving, wasn't dissolving.

Fear clutched Leon deep. He couldn't pass through the time stream without Noel. They had to be together for him to survive.

"Noel!" he screamed.

Then, there was nothing.

CHAPTER 10

∞

Sweat-drenched and frightened, Noel battled himself awake. He sat upright as though catapulted, then gasped as rivers of fire inflamed his ribs.

Cool hands touched his face, his brow. A gentle voice said, *"Suavemente, suavemente, por favor."*

The mists clouding his vision cleared away. He squinted into the broad, homely face of an unknown woman. Her brown face was shiny with sweat. Her graying hair was plaited in two neat braids that hung down to her plump shoulders. Her eyes, a dark compassionate brown, met his with concern.

"Please, señor, lie still. You will open the cuts and bleed again."

He did not know where he was. His bed was a massive thing carved of dark wood. A tester overhead was draped with heavy, dust-coated velvet. The tall sides and footboard made him feel as though he'd been enclosed in an airless box. The room was all shadows and gloom, with tiny slivers of sunlight leaking through closed shutters on the windows. Stuffy heat sat on him like a weight.

She pressed him down, and although her strong hands were

gentle he could not help but wince as his back touched the sheets.

"Is bad," she said softly in English, rolling him onto his side and propping him with pillows. "Is bad, but you must sleep again. Is the only way to heal."

He shivered, suddenly cold, and she put a cup of cool water to his lips. He drank some of it, then grew tired. She took the cup away and sat humming beside the bed, the way a nanny might croon to children. Noel closed his eyes but he was afraid to sleep, afraid the nightmare would come back.

It did.

His own screams woke him up. He opened his eyes, panting and trembling, to find his flailing arms caught in a strong grip. Don Emilio held his wrists.

Noel shuddered and drew a deep breath, realizing he was still in the bed like a box. "No Indians," he murmured weakly and slumped against his pillows.

Don Emilio released his wrists. "No, my friend," he said. "There are no Indians here. Have some water."

He held the cup and supported Noel's head while he drank. Soothed, Noel rested a moment, watching as Don Emilio put the empty silver cup upon the bedside table and pulled a chair close. The shadows in the room had changed. They were darker in the corners. Only night stood behind the closed wooden shutters now. A silver candelabrum held three burning candles. Their light flickered a soft gold over Don Emilio's clasped hands, which rested on the edge of the bed. His face and shoulders remained in shadow.

"You have given us much worry," said Don Emilio. "But I think you are beginning to be a little better now."

Noel frowned. He was still confused, and the effort to make sense of things seemed too great. Still, he tried. "I'm not home."

"No, you are at my hacienda. In fact, you are in my bed. It

is the best in the house, and you are welcome to it for being such a brave fool."

There were several emotions running beneath Don Emilio's light tone. Noel felt too tired to sort through them.

"Cody and I brought you here three days ago. Do you remember? No? *Bueno.* I think it is better you do not. The journey, slung across my horse, was a harsh one. We did not think you would live."

"Lisa-Marie?"

Don Emilio shifted, and the candlelight revealed his smile. "Ah, she is almost recovered from her ordeal. We let her walk today for a little while. Her feet are much better. Tomorrow, she will come and visit you."

He reached out and gripped Noel's hand. His fingers were strong and dry. His aristocratic face still smiled a little, but there was no amusement in his hazel eyes. "Thank you, amigo," he whispered hoarsely. "You saved her life, when I did not think any of us would succeed in rescuing her from the Apaches. She has told us what you did. In private, I will say that I am in your debt for this act of courage. She is not of my family, but in this land all ranching people must stick together."

He was speaking with two meanings again. Noel knew he needed his wits about him in dealing with this complex man, but right now it was all he could do to keep his eyes open.

"Are you going to marry her?" he asked.

Don Emilio blinked. For a moment his urbane mask slipped, and astonishment showed through. "I—what a question you ask me! *Sangre de Cristo,* I do not think we need discuss such a thing right now."

"But you've thought about it," persisted Noel.

"How do you know this?" asked Don Emilio with narrowed eyes. He cocked his head to one side. "This is a thought that has barely crossed my mind this afternoon while having tea with the señorita, and already you know it. Do you read minds perhaps?"

"No, my brother does that," said Noel before he could stop himself. He was aghast at the slip, but Don Emilio only laughed.

"Yes, you are improved, if you can make jokes. I only wish we could find your brother."

Noel frowned. "Where is he? You mean you let him get away?"

Don Emilio spread his hands. "He was gone when we found you and Lisa-Marie. She was almost fainting of thirst and hunger. The poor child was delirious. She kept babbling about ghosts and, oh, such things as make no sense. You were . . . well, as you know. Leon left no tracks for us to follow. That *diablo* will pay for the trouble he has caused."

"He's gone?" repeated Noel, unable to understand. "But I saw him with us. He was afraid. I made him afraid to go off by himself. He . . ." A wave of coldness washed through Noel. He put his fingers to his face. "I feel strange."

"Ah," said Don Emilio, rising to his feet. "I have kept you talking too long. Now you are tired. You must sleep."

"No—"

"Yes, yes, it is important for you to regain your health quickly." Don Emilio glanced over his shoulder and snapped his fingers.

At once a slim, gray-haired man in black came forward from where he had been hidden in the shadows. He bowed to Don Emilio and began stirring a potion in a glass. Don Emilio walked to the door.

"Good night, my friend. We will talk more tomorrow."

Alarmed by some instinct he could not place, Noel sat up. At once the pain came roaring through him, and half-closed cuts opened to let air sting through his wounds. The welts on his bare skin were purplish and crimson, and throbbed mercilessly. Around him, the room seemed to tilt and lean in. He felt a coldness inside him that had nothing to do with anything else.

It was as though a piece of him was missing. He frowned, unable to put his finger on what was wrong.

Then he looked at his wrists and realized the LOC was missing.

"My LOC!" he said sharply, then corrected himself. "My bracelet, the one of Indian silver, where is it?" As he spoke, he felt anger growing. If Leon had stolen his LOC again, he would regret it.

The doctor had clammy hands and dirty fingernails. "Easy, señor," he said. "You must drink this. It will ease the pain and your fever."

Noel shoved his hand away hard enough to make the black liquid slosh over the rim of the glass. "Get that away from me. Where is my—"

"Noel, amigo, be still," said Don Emilio. He picked up the bracelet from the top of a chest standing near the door. "Here are all your possessions. Nothing is lost. Now drink your laudanum and rest."

Relief went through Noel, but he refused to give way to it. He held out his hand. "Give it to me. I want it on my wrist."

Don Emilio glanced at the doctor and shrugged. "Of course," he said, coming to Noel and slipping the heavy silver cuff onto Noel's wrist. "If it will make you feel better. Now it is with you. *Bueno.* Take the medicine."

"No." said Noel. He felt sweat break out across him. The effort to keep sitting up became too great. Pain throbbed and roared across his senses. "No drugs. I'll sleep without them."

"Señor," said the doctor in concern. "The laudanum is very mild. You will not become addicted. This I swear. But without it you will have no rest."

Noel's gaze sought Don Emilio's. "Get him out of here. I don't want it."

Don Emilio hesitated, then he nodded and ushered the protesting doctor from the room. Noel sank back gingerly, trying to find a comfortable position in vain. By gradual degrees the tension drained from him. Small wonder he was having horrible nightmares, when they had him toked to the eyebrows on an opium derivative.

Travelers were injected with implants and symbiotics to protect them from untreated water, primitive sanitation conditions, tainted food, and the like. They were supposed to avoid ingesting anything—such as local medicines—that might upset the precise balance of protection created within their own system.

Noel flexed his left wrist, glad to have his LOC back. Now that it was on his arm again, the implant-triggered alarm eased off.

Don Emilio closed the door on the still-protesting doctor and returned to Noel's bedside. "You are stubborn. There is no need to be brave now. Why not make your suffering comfortable?"

"No," said Noel grimly.

Don Emilio shrugged. "As you wish. Would you like some more water?"

"Please."

The Mexican filled the silver cup from an ewer. Noel watched him carefully to make sure there were no tricks. Before he drank he even sniffed suspiciously.

Don Emilio laughed. "*Dios!* How you mistrust us all. Drops are for old women, eh? Now drink and go to sleep. Someone will stay near in case you decide to be less brave in the night."

Noel drank the well water and let his head sink deep into the soft feather pillow. Don Emilio blew out the candles, and

SHOWDOWN

darkness folded over the room like a blanket.

When the heavy door closed behind him, Noel waited a few moments, then roused himself from the edges of unconsciousness.

"LOC," he said softly, "activate."

The bracelet shimmered into its true shape, and the light emanating from its circuitry cast an eerie glow about the room.

"Scan," said Noel. "Locate Leon."

"Duplicate not found."

"What?" Noel blinked, not certain he'd heard correctly. "Explain not found."

"Duplicate does not register in scan."

"Is he out of range?"

"Negative."

"Where is he then?"

The LOC did not answer.

"LOC," said Noel more sharply, "run hypothesis. Where is the duplicate?"

The LOC hummed for a long while. Noel struggled to keep his eyes open. There was something wrong. He felt strange, unsettled in a way he could not describe more precisely. He didn't think this feeling came from the laudanum he'd been given earlier.

"If he's gone to join El Raton, we'll—"

"Negative," said the LOC.

"Specify reply. Do you mean he isn't with El Raton or—"

"Negative existence."

Noel was stunned. "You mean he's gone? Really gone? He doesn't exist anymore? Not anywhere?"

"Negative existence."

It seemed too good to be true. Noel grinned to himself. "At last!" he said. "He's finally out of my hair. Good riddance."

"Negative placement in fourth dimension. Inverted time stream. Time loop widening. Danger."

"Wait a minute," said Noel. "Danger? What danger? What do you mean, the time loop is widening? It can't do that, unless there's something going wrong on the other side." In excitement, he propped himself up on one elbow.

"LOC," he commanded, "run diagnostic scan into time stream. Verify malfunctions. Specifically: Is a malfunction happening at origin point? Can the malfunction be terminated from this side? Can the malfunction be kept from reaching you? How far is the time stream inverting? Will it affect events taking place here? Run."

"Running," said the LOC.

It hummed a long while, so long it grew warm on his wrist. Noel wiped the perspiration from his forehead and allowed himself to lie down again. He was growing so tired he could barely concentrate.

"Danger," said the LOC. "Possibility seventy-nine percent that you will be pulled into the time stream."

"How?" said Noel. "By wearing you?"

"Negative. Through link to duplicate."

Noel frowned and decided he wanted to chew on that a while. "Answer my other questions. I might as well know the worst all at once."

"Malfunction affirmative. Origin point confirmed. Origin point scanning down time stream in search-mode logistical pattern."

Noel chuckled and slapped the bed. "Looking for me, by God!"

"Affirmative. Inversion increasing by exponential factor seven—"

"Stop," said Noel. So finally someone back at the Time Institute had decided he was lost, and they were looking for him. Maybe they could fish him back. But the inversion shouldn't be happening. That was an effect of the linear time stream curling back on itself, thus widening. If the time stream widened too far, it could dissipate, thus causing . . .

Noel frowned. He didn't want to think about all the theories of what might happen in such a situation. Tampering with the fourth dimension was a tricky business at best, requiring precision and a delicate respect for the parallels of history and events. Too much interference with time, and the paradox occurred. The whole future could be wiped out, changed irrevocably. Dimensions could be altered. The chaos from this would be incalculable.

He drew in a sharp breath. "Maybe it's not the Time Institute looking for us. Me, I mean. Maybe the anarchists who damaged you in the first place have taken over. Now they're trying to sabotage all of time. Can you verify that, LOC?"

"Negative. Origin point only."

"Damn." He gnawed on his bottom lip a while. Rescue or destruction? Gambling had never been something he enjoyed. And fifty-fifty odds were lousy.

"Can you block it?" he asked, knowing even as he posed the question that the LOC might cut them off and trap them here forever.

The LOC pulsed. "Affirmative. Scan can be blocked."

"Then—"

"Danger. Time stream is wider. Inversion close to—"

"Stop," said Noel. "Can you scan all the way to origin point?"

"Affirmative. Already in—"

"Stop. Can you open communications line?"

"Negative. That function is damaged."

"I know. I thought maybe you'd repaired yourself while you weren't doing anything else."

"Self-repair in that mode is not possible."

"That's what you always say. Can you scan all the way to origin point?"

"Affirmative."

Noel considered it. The Institute's equipment would register if it was scanned. They could trace the scan to its origin, in this case his LOC, and pinpoint his time and location. During the twentieth-century submarine warfare, boat commanders sometimes communicated with sonar pings. The scan would be his ping, telling the Institute he was alive.

Excitement built inside him. He tried to remind himself that if the anarchists had succeeded in taking over the Institute, there would be no rescue ever.

However, anything was better than remaining in this helpless limbo of a closed time loop.

He drew a deep breath. "Scan to origin point."

"Working."

The LOC hummed a moment, then flashed violently. "Scan blocked. Danger. Scan blocked. Danger. Scan—"

"Stop," said Noel hastily before it could burn itself out. "Analyze. What is blocking the scan?"

"Duplicate in time stream. Inversion widening. Danger."

Again Noel was aware of the coldness inside him, the coldness that was like the void between dimensions. Was he, too, going to slip into nowhere just when rescue might finally be about to happen?

"Damn him," said Noel savagely. "Cut the link."

"Not possible."

"Then how do we get him out of the way?"

While the LOC analyzed the problem, Noel rammed his fingers through his hair. He needed a shave. He was hungry. He felt like hell. If Leon had ruined their chance to get back, he'd . . .

It did no good to finish the threat in his mind. There was

nothing he could imagine that would be harsh enough for what Leon deserved.

"Come on, LOC. Come on!"

"Affirmative," said the LOC.

That was not the expected reply. Noel frowned, afraid the LOC was starting to overheat or perhaps malfunction.

"Reply to specific questions," he said. "How do we get him back?"

"Affirmative."

"LOC! Reset response mode. Reply directly to specific question as follows: How do we get duplicate out of inverted time stream?"

The lights within the LOC flickered, then resumed their steady pulsing. "Response: Enter inverted time stream and relink."

"What?"

"Response: Enter inverted—"

"Stop," said Noel. He lay sweating on his pillows and closed his eyes. The prospect scared him. Going into the time stream without a destination code locked in was like walking outside a space shuttle without a tether.

Resentment choked his throat. Why did Leon always cause trouble?

But dwelling on how exasperating his duplicate was brought Noel no closer to a solution. He forced open his weary eyes. The decision had to be made.

"Let me state the situation," he said. "I can remain here and do nothing. There will be no contact made, no rescue back to my own time. I will probably lose Leon forever if he remains trapped in the time stream. *Or,* I can attempt to drag Leon back to this reality and then scan to origin point in hopes of eventual rescue."

"Affirmative," said the LOC. "Note additional possibility to be factored into choice A: probability of duplicate pulling you into time stream is eighty-nine point five percent. Link may not be broken."

"Yeah," said Noel dryly. "I'd better remember that. If I decide to enter the inversion, can it be done? Can you take me there?"

"Destination code?"

"No destination code."

The LOC hummed. "Destination code?"

Noel sighed. Safety features were great until you needed to dispense with them and found you couldn't. "Forget destination codes," he snapped. "Yours don't work, remember?"

"Destination code?"

"Leon!" he said in exasperation. "Destination is Leon, my duplicate. Can you send me to him?"

"Affirmative."

"Can you get us out?"

"Widening time stream is causing variables in predictions. Calculations state a sixty-six percent possibility of—"

"Don't tell me the odds," said Noel. "Do it," he said before he could lose his nerve. "Engage travel."

The LOC pulsed brightly. It grew uncomfortably warm on his wrist. The room blurred around him, and he felt himself dissolving into the mist of nowhere.

With an abrupt, wrenching lurch, he snapped back into reality and hit the bed with a thud that brought a cry to his lips. He bit it back just in time, for he didn't want to arouse the rest of the household and have them coming in here to check on him.

What the hell had gone wrong? he wondered. He opened his mouth to ask the LOC, but before he could speak blackness engulfed him, a blackness so cold and silent it terrified him. He knew then that he had slipped between dimensions, into that dangerous place of nowhere. In ordinary travel, *between* lasted only scant seconds, hardly longer than a heartbeat.

But this was lasting longer. He had ceased to exist corporeally. He lacked sight, hearing, smell, feel. Without some reference point to cling to, he felt the edges of his mind disintegrating. Madness could happen so easily here.

He forced himself to focus quickly on Leon. Bit by bit he built an image of his duplicate in his mind, assembling that visage so like his own, yet different. He was thankful for every tiny difference, every minute alteration in the bone structure, in the width of the mouth, in the color of the eyes. They were not the same. They were *not* one.

"Leon!" he called without a voice.

Something replied, a voice that was not a voice. It was more a ripple in the void surrounding Noel. He felt a sensation of rushing, as though a wind passed through him. For a split second, he felt complete. He felt Leon's mind merging with his. He welcomed it, for they were complete again as they should be, two halves of the same entity.

He relaxed in that sensation, letting them become one. Leon was warmth in the coldness of nothing. Noel delighted in him for the first time. He shared himself eagerly, anxious to make their union permanent, keeping no guard raised now.

The wind swirled and rushed through him, and then with a jolt the wind left. Noel felt ripped in half again. A terrible agony seized him.

"Leon!" he cried. "Stay with me!"

A trace of mocking laughter coiled through his mind. With it came Leon's voice: "Now *you* need *me*."

Betrayed yet again, Noel wondered how he could have ever considered them two halves of the same whole. Leon was *not* part of him. No, he was something else, something twisted and horrifying. And now, knowing how important his return was, he chose instead to destroy them both.

Fury filled Noel, a throbbing ferocious emotion greater than he could contain. It swelled through him, overwhelmed him. He lost coherent thought. He tried to hurl himself after the wind, but it was gone, gone forever. He was only a speck spinning in infinity, alone.

CHAPTER 11

∞

Noel jolted back to reality in time to see a hand coming down over his face. Thinking he was about to be smothered in his sleep, he let out a yell and sat up.

The priest jerked back his hand and hastily crossed himself. "Santa Maria," he breathed, pale and wide-eyed.

Blinking, Noel looked around and found he was still in the boxlike bed. Candles burned at the head and foot, making him feel like he was in a funeral parlor. The air was stuffy with the scents of incense and unwashed clothes. On the opposite side of the bed, a tear-streaked Lisa-Marie rose to her feet with her mouth open in astonishment.

"Noel," she said.

"It cannot be," whispered the priest.

Noel glared at the priest, who was skinny, young, and nervous. His long black cassock was dust-stained. He wore his green stole about his neck and held a small vial in one shaking hand.

"What's going on? What were you doing to me?" demanded Noel.

"Extreme unction—"

"The last rites?" broke in Noel. "What for? I'm fine."

The priest merely stared at him and backed away from the bed. He had grown so pale his eyes looked stark. "A— a miracle," he whispered.

Lisa-Marie flung her arms around Noel's neck and wept. "You're alive. You're alive."

He pulled free, wincing. "Yes, of course I'm alive. What is all this?"

But even as he asked he was beginning to figure it out. He sighed, feeling tired and grouchy. The attempt to regain Leon had failed. Now he wasn't certain he could contact the Institute at all, and he couldn't try as long as these people were in the room.

"Oh, Noel, I can't believe it," said Lisa-Marie softly. Her blue eyes glowed. "I prayed and prayed, and now you're all right. I guess faith does work. Oh, I'm so happy! I just knew that if you died I would die too."

"Now wait a minute—"

She gripped his arm. "After all you did, after all you went through to save me . . . well, I've never known anyone could be so brave. Now I'm going to do everything for you, nurse you back to health and—"

"I don't need nursing," said Noel, pulling free of her again. He eyed her with growing alarm. She had all the markings of a teenage girl lost to infatuation and hero worship. That was the last kind of problem he needed right now. "Thanks just the same, but I'd like some privacy."

She smiled deep into his eyes. "Yes, of course, Noel. Whatever you say. I'll run and tell the others. They'll be so glad. And I'll get you a tray of food. You must be famished. Oh, Noel, I cried and cried over you. And now I'm so happy I think I could fly!"

She kissed him on the cheek, and blushed rosily before rushing from the room. Meanwhile, the priest seemed to have regained some of his composure.

"You were dead, señor," he whispered. "Now you are alive. How can this be?"

Inwardly Noel groaned. Inversion traveling with his mind had left his body in a deep trance. No wonder he felt like he'd been through a wringer. In a sense he had been. Splitting mind and body was tough work. Men weren't designed to be wrenched apart and slapped back together that way. But he couldn't explain anything truthful to the priest, and he wasn't in the mood to invent an explanation.

"Look," he said, knowing he should take the time to reassure this man but not having the patience for it, "I was asleep, not dead. You shouldn't be so quick to jump to conclusions."

"The doctor said you were dead."

"The doctor is a quack," said Noel, shoving his hair back with his fingers. "He doesn't wash his hands often enough, and I bet he's never heard of germs or carbolic acid."

"Señor?" said the priest in bewilderment.

"Just go away, will you?" said Noel. He swung his legs off the bed and tried standing up. His knees were as weak as a newborn colt's. He grabbed the side of the bed for support, wincing as his welts stung.

The priest muttered something and fled the room. Noel could hear him shouting hysterically. In exasperation, Noel staggered across the room, hitching up his linen underdrawers as he went, and shut the heavy wooden door. By the time he locked it, someone was knocking.

Afraid it was Lisa-Marie, Noel turned away from the door and activated his LOC. "Make contact with origin point," he said urgently. "Scan origin point now."

"Scanning."

Noel grinned to himself with relief. That meant Leon was out of the time stream. Maybe this hadn't been a complete waste after all. He didn't know where his duplicate had gone to, and he really didn't care, as long as he could get home.

"Well?" he said impatiently. "Are you making contact?"

The LOC hummed without replying.

The knocking grew more insistent. "Noel?" said Lisa-Marie. "Noel, are you all right? Please unlock the door."

Noel ignored her. "LOC, respond! Are you making contact?"

"Negative."

The hope left him like air escaping a pricked balloon. He rubbed his face and almost felt like giving up. "Explain," he said quietly.

"Scan into time stream from origin point no longer occurring."

"You're saying they can't pick up our scan unless they are scanning themselves?"

"Affirmative. Time stream has narrowed. Inversion is down to twenty-five percent and dropping."

"Yippee," muttered Noel, then decided he needn't wallow in self-pity. "I guess we succeeded in wiping out that danger. Is Leon out of the time stream?"

"Scanning . . . affirmative."

Noel blinked in surprise. "He is? But I didn't hold him with me. And we didn't come back together."

"Coexistence not possible."

The knocking came again, hard enough to make the key rattle in the keyhole. "Señor!" called a masculine voice. "Señor, are you there?"

Noel frowned. It was hard to think with all that noise going on. He walked away from the door. "We usually don't come through the time stream together. I don't know why I expected it this time. I thought we'd be rejoined or something."

"Coexistence not possible."

"But aren't we halves?"

"Negative. Anomaly in the first time stream created a duplicate. No damage was done to original."

"Yeah, me. I'm the original." Noel sighed. "Still, all this boils down to is I missed my chance to get back."

Something heavy was thudding against the door now, making the hinges groan as though the people outside were trying to break it down.

Noel pulled himself together. He couldn't lose hope now. If the Institute had scanned once, they might scan again. "LOC, maintain scan to origin point. If the Institute tries to look for us again, I want you to make contact with them."

"Acknowledged."

"Resume disguise mode."

The LOC shimmered briefly and took on the shape of the silver and turquoise cuff. Noel returned to the door, which was creaking and shuddering beneath the onslaught on the other side.

"All right. All *right!*" he said in irritation and turned the key. He jumped back hastily in time to avoid being knocked down as the door slammed open and crashed against the plastered wall. The crucifix fell to the floor.

Don Emilio, the doctor, the priest, and two burly servants in white cotton shirts and trousers stood crowded in the doorway. Lisa-Marie was not in evidence, much to Noel's relief.

"You see? You see?" said the priest hysterically. "I did not lie."

Don Emilio was the first to recover his composure. Dressed in a short jacket of dark blue velvet and trousers sporting a row of silver buttons down the sides, he stepped forward. His hazel eyes frowned in bewilderment. "You appear to be much recovered, my friend. This is *bueno.*"

"Well, thanks," said Noel. "All I know is I went to sleep and when I woke up this fellow was smearing oil on my face. I'm not Catholic, by the way," he added.

The priest's brows shot up. He looked affronted. "And the medallion of Mary found in your pocket?"

"Not mine," said Noel.

The priest glared at him and jerked off his stole. "If you will please excuse me, Don Emilio. I will collect my bag and depart."

Don Emilio stepped aside and let the priest gather the paraphernalia he had left on the bedside table. When he passed Noel, however, the priest suddenly held up the cross he wore on a long chain around his neck and touched Noel's shoulder with a probing fingertip.

Noel met his eyes. "I'm not a ghost."

"A miracle," said the priest. Shaking his head, he left the room.

"May I?" asked the doctor.

"No," said Noel sharply before Don Emilio could reply. "I'm fine."

"Perhaps a brief coma induced by—"

"—too much laudanum," snapped Noel. "Look, I was tired. I needed some sleep. I can't help it if you thought I was dead. Maybe you should go home and reread your medical textbooks."

Flustered, the doctor departed. Don Emilio smiled, although his eyes remained troubled.

"You are very short of temper this evening."

Noel ran his fingers through his hair. "Sorry. It's been a rough day."

"My friend, you have been *asleep* for nearly two days. We could not rouse you. After a period of several hours you stopped breathing. The priest was late in arriving or he would have administered the rites sooner." Don Emilio hesitated. "If you are not Catholic, why do you carry a medallion?"

Noel allowed himself to sit down on the edge of the bed. He wondered where his clothes were. "It's a long story."

"We were going to bury you at dawn," said Don Emilio.

Startled, Noel looked up at him.

"Yes," said Don Emilio softly. "Lucky for you that you awoke in time."

Noel thought about coming out of the inverted time stream to find himself trapped in a pine coffin six feet under. Small, dark places had never been his favorite. He shuddered.

Don Emilio opened a tall armoire of heavily carved walnut and took out a decanter and a pair of glasses. "For a man who recently suffered fever, perhaps brandy is not good. But I need some for myself. Will you join me?"

Brandy on an empty stomach. "Sure," said Noel. He accepted a glass of the amber liquid. It slid like mellow fire all the way down. He sighed. In the twenty-sixth century, fine old cognac—as well as most wines—were synthesized mixes. No one possessed the land or the patience to grow, bottle, and ferment according to the old methods.

"When's dinner?" asked Noel.

Don Emilio laughed. "Ah, now I believe it is true. A ghost does not get hungry, eh? Do you feel up to getting dressed, or do you wish a servant to bring a tray here to your room?"

Before Noel could answer, Lisa-Marie came hurrying inside. Behind her walked an elderly servant with a tray laden with food. Noel muttered an oath and pulled the bedcovers to his waist. He noticed she had managed to pin up her hair into a soft chignon that made her look older, and she had changed into a pale blue dress with ruffles on the bodice. A shawl of delicate lace hung off her shoulders.

"Isn't it wonderful, Don Emilio?" she said, her eyes only for Noel. "All my prayers were answered."

Don Emilio raised his brows. "Er, yes," he said carefully. "We are of course delighted that Señor Kedran is so much better."

"Cody doesn't believe me," she said, tossing her head. "I told him to come and see for himself, just as soon as you've eaten."

"I think perhaps it is better not to rush things," said Don Emilio sternly. "Visitors tomorrow."

"But why?" she asked, gazing at Noel with an incandescent smile that almost made him lose interest in the aromatic food being uncovered by the servant. "Cody likes him too. After all, Noel saved both our lives. Only, I think my rescue was more dramatic. I mean you nearly *died* yourself on my behalf, Noel. I can never forget that. Nor can I forget what I owe—"

"You don't owe me anything," said Noel sharply. "Leon caused the trouble. I was just taking care of it."

She lifted her chin and gave him a smoldering look. "You're very modest, Noel."

He nearly choked on a bite of tamale. Coughing, he reached for his glass, but she was quicker to pick it up. She handed it to him with a smile. Gulping the wine, he shot Don Emilio a glance of appeal.

Don Emilio, however, was watching Lisa-Marie with a frown and did not notice.

Lisa-Marie took the knife and fork from Noel's hands. "Let me cut your food for you."

He snatched the utensils back. "I can cut my own. I'm not an invalid."

"Let me pour some more wine for you."

He took his glass from her hand, causing her to spill the wine. "I've got enough."

"Oh, dear. I've spilled wine on your food. Let me get you some more."

Exasperated, he thrust the whole tray at her. "Please do."

She smiled, and made sure their fingers touched as she took the tray. "I'll be right back."

He smiled in return until the door closed behind her, then he threw off the bedcovers. "Where are my trousers? Lock the door, would you please, Don Emilio? And for God's sake don't let her back in."

Don Emilio did not stir from where he stood with his shoulder leaning against the armoire. "It must be pleasant to have the adoration of such a lovely young señorita."

Noel grimaced. "Wrong. The last thing I need is to be chased by a girl young enough to be my daughter."

"Chased? You use an unkind word, my friend. You imply that she is less than a lady."

"She's a child."

Don Emilio almost smiled. "Hardly. She is on the verge of womanhood, and you have not been kind to her. If you hurt her, then—"

"I'm not going to hurt her," said Noel, shoving his hand through his hair. "I'm not going to do anything to her. All I want is to find my pants."

"And then what will you do?"

Noel pointed at the shutters. "Climb out that window."

Don Emilio laughed. The sound was rich and full-throated. Amusement returned to his hazel eyes. "I can see the little dove does not have your heart."

Noel stopped rummaging in the chest and glared at him. "Of course she doesn't. Didn't I suggest once before that you marry her? I mean, you're not married already or anything like that?"

"We have had this conversation before. Why do you insist?"

Noel wished he could explain. But he figured he was already strange enough to these people without claiming he could see into the future. "I, uh, just think it would be wise."

"In the business sense, perhaps. It would soothe an old emnity reaching back thirty years. You see, the Double T was once part of my father's rancho before the Americans took it for their own territory. Many times my father tried to reclaim this land. I regret to say that some of his methods were unscrupulous. He and Señor Trask became bitter enemies. I myself have no quarrel with the old man, except that I, too, would like to have the land back under the Navarres name. I have offered many times to buy it, but the old man will not sell."

"Did you hire El Raton to burn him out?" asked Noel.

He might as well have thrown oil on a burning fire. Don Emilio's eyes blazed.

"You dare accuse me of that! I will have you know that if I wanted to use the methods of *bandidos* I would not need the riffraff El Raton leads. No, my own men could force the Trasks off their land. They could shoot all the Double T cattle. They could poison the water holes. They could cut down the fences. Yes, and then the Yankee soldiers would come, and perhaps America and Mexico would have another war."

Noel's clothes were folded neatly in the bottom of the armoire. He put his trousers on in silence and decided his back was still too sore to endure the shirt. While he fiddled with the clothes, he avoided looking at Don Emilio. The silence spun out in the room, then someone knocked at the door.

"Noel?" called Lisa-Marie's voice. "I'm back."

Noel groaned. He glanced at Don Emilio and made one last try. "If you married her, you'd not only have a beautiful wife, but you would have her grandfather's ranch . . . eventually."

Don Emilio's brows drew together. "You are confused, my friend. There is her uncle—"

"He may be dead by now."

"And there is her brother. She will not inherit."

"She might—"

"No, no. Stop this. I am a ruthless man. It is necessary in order to run a rancho as large as mine. But I am not without principles. To coldly plot the life of this young girl, to take her solely for my own monetary gain—no, I am not that desperate."

"But I thought arranged marriages were common in this century." Too late Noel realized what he'd blurted out.

Don Emilio gave him a peculiar look. "True, it is often the custom for parents to make the marriage arrangements. But Thomas Trask would never agree to give me his granddaughter's hand, even if I asked for it."

"Just what's so special about the Double T anyway?"

Lisa-Marie knocked on the door. "Noel? Are you all right? Aren't you going to let me back in?"

Don Emilio said, "Aren't you going to let her back in?"

"No," said Noel. "Why is the ranch so important?"

"Sentiment. It once belonged to us."

He was lying, Noel realized. Noel shook his head. "It's small, isn't it?"

"*Sí*, not even ten sections."

"And you already have how many?"

Don Emilio shrugged and poured himself some more brandy. "If you were to stand on the rooftop in the morning, as far as you could see in any direction would be my land."

"Yeah, that's what I thought. Hundreds of sections, thousands of acres . . . so why the Double T? You shouldn't even miss it, yet your father nearly caused a war trying to get it back, and you keep raising your offers every year."

"It is rude to ask such insistent, personal questions," said Don Emilio coldly. "You are a guest beneath my roof, and that gives you many liberties, but I warn you not to push into matters that are not your concern."

"It is my concern," said Noel. "I'm not going to explain how, but I have an important stake in how this comes out. If you don't tell me, I'll persist until I have the answer."

"My peons will tell you nothing. They are completely loyal to me."

"Sure they are."

Don Emilio gripped his arm hard, and his hazel eyes bored into Noel's with a menace that was unmistakable. "I have warned you once. I shall not do so again. Do not meddle. *Buenas noches.*"

He walked out past Lisa-Marie, who was still waiting for admittance. The elderly servant stood patiently at her heels with a fresh tray.

They came in together. Lisa-Marie chattered incessantly while Noel ate, but he paid her no attention. Before he was finished, Cody came hesitantly to the doorway and peeped in.

"Cody!" said Lisa-Marie. "Come on in. Can you believe how well he looks? It's just a miracle."

Cody turned so red his freckles disappeared. He scuffed his boot toe shyly on the tiled floor. "We sure were worried about you. The way everyone was acting around here, I figured you were a goner."

"Well, I'm not," said Noel, polishing off the last of his refried beans with a folded piece of tortilla. "Thanks, Lisa-Marie. That was delicious."

She beamed at him, and he glanced at Cody to keep from being blinded. "Come in. I have some questions to ask."

Cody shuffled in, still red-faced and tongue-tied. "We owe you a lot—"

"Now don't you start," said Noel hastily and switched the subject. "Do you know why Don Emilio wants your grandfather's ranch?"

The twins suddenly looked very much alike. Even Lisa-Marie lost some of her glow. They exchanged a quick look, then faced Noel and shook their heads.

He sighed. They were lying to him too. He decided to take off the kid gloves. "Okay, you two," he said sharply. "You keep saying how much you owe me for saving your lives, *both* your lives. So pay up by telling me the truth."

Lisa-Marie set her jaw stubbornly and stared into the distance.

Cody met Noel's gaze briefly and grimaced. "I'm sorry," he said. "We can't."

"Cody," she said in warning.

He shrugged. "We gave our word to Grandpa."

"Which is more important, your debt to me or your promise to the old man?"

Cody stared at him in shock, and even Lisa-Marie looked as though her hero-worship was fading fast.

"That's an awful thing to ask," whispered Cody hoarsely.

Noel went on staring at him. "There are choices in life. Some of them are unpleasant."

"Now you sound like Skeet."

"Good old Skeet," said Lisa-Marie as though eager to change the subject. "I wish you had stayed with him, Cody, instead of hooking up with Don Emilio. Now look at the mess we're in."

"What mess?" said Noel quickly.

"Nothing," said Cody.

"He's keeping us here and won't let us go home," said Lisa-Marie. "He wants Grandpa to come here. I guess he's trying to make Grandpa feel beholding to him for rescuing us. But Don Emilio didn't save us. You did, Noel."

Noel sighed. The chances for nuptials were getting slimmer all the time. "That's right. But Don Emilio's not so bad. He's been kind and—"

"Yeah, the way a snake coils up afore it strikes!" said Cody.

"Before," said Lisa-Marie. "*Before* it strikes. Cody, you're sounding more and more illiterate."

"And you're pretty stuck up these days," he retorted.

"Children, stop it," said Noel.

That got their attention. Both of them glared at him.

"We are not children," said Lisa-Marie icily.

"Then don't act like it. And let's get back to your grandfather's ranch. Why does Don Emilio want it so much?"

The twins stared at each other a moment, and Noel got the impression they were communing.

"We *promised*," said Lisa-Marie.

"Yeah, and maybe it's time we thought about that promise. If Noel can help us—"

"But will he?"

Tired of listening to their argument, Noel cleared his throat and raised his brows.

Lisa-Marie sent him a sharp look and said, "I guess I trust you."

"Well, thanks," he said, irritated. "Considering I've given you every reason to so far—"

"You don't understand," she broke in with a blush that made her look very pretty indeed. He wondered if she could do that at will. "You see, I think you're perfectly wonderful, but Uncle Frank taught us to always make certain a man has all his cards on the table. Don Emilio is handsome and charming, but we know he's a snake."

"He sure is," said Cody. "A double-tongued, double-dealing, two-faced, underhanded, great big snake in the grass. I never could see why Uncle Frank fuzzed up like an old tomcat whenever Don Emilio came by the house, but now that he's keeping us prisoners here I understand. It's like a ransom or something. I don't like him having Grandpa over a barrel."

"Okay, okay," said Noel. "I get the message. You want to make a deal with me, right?"

"That's right," said Lisa-Marie sweetly. "If we tell you why Don Emilio wants our ranch, you have to help us escape—"

"—and get home to Grandpa and Uncle Frank," said Cody.

"—and get home," said Lisa-Marie. She smiled radiantly at Noel and batted her lashes. She looked innocent and demure, but she was just as stubborn and flint-hearted as the rest of the Trasks. "Is it a deal, Noel?"

Noel hesitated, his old training about noninvolvement coming to the fore. His training was to be an observer, to stand aside from the events of history and merely record them for analysis and example in his own time. But since his LOC had been sabotaged, he found himself unable to avoid meddling. The last time it had been Leon who changed history, and Noel had to work hard to change it back. This time he had changed history himself by saving Cody from drowning. It was beginning to look like he had changed things for the better, because no matter how much he told himself not to interfere or alter history, he couldn't see letting this boy die just so his sister could marry a man who didn't love her. Maybe the LOC was mistaken. Maybe its data banks had been damaged, and it was feeding him false information.

Noel flinched from the thought. If he lost faith in his LOC, then he lost all hope of ever getting back.

"Well?" said Lisa-Marie.

"Well?" said Cody.

Shoulder to shoulder, they stared at him with identical intensity in their blue eyes.

Noel frowned. If he helped this pair escape Don Emilio, then it looked like his change of history was going to stand. That violated his code, his ethics, his oath as a traveler.

Noel rose to his feet. "It's a deal."

CHAPTER 12

∞

"Mighty fine!" said Cody with enthusiasm. "Let's go—"

"Wait a minute," said Noel sharply. "You tell me what I want to know first."

"Nope," said Cody. "We'll tell you when we're safely away from the hacienda and on our way to the border."

Noel sat down, wincing as the waistband of his trousers rubbed across a low-reaching welt. "You're going to have to trust me, Cody."

Cody's face wrinkled with uncertainty, the way it had when he'd chosen to go with Don Emilio instead of Skeet. "I do, Noel, but it's just—"

"I'm being treated fine here," said Noel. "Why should I be rude to my host and sneak out?"

"Now you're trying to hold us over a barrel," began Cody hotly, but Lisa-Marie put her hand on his forearm.

"Cody, hush up," she said. "We've already made the deal. Go close the door."

Muttering, Cody did so. Lisa-Marie faced Noel and said in a low, rapid voice, "There's a large vein of silver that runs diagonally through the Double T. It's pretty much played out on the south side of the border. Don Emilio's father mined it heavily. Now he wants ours."

"Why isn't your grandfather mining it?" asked Noel.

"Access," said Cody. "We got no railroad close by. Not close enough for a spur to be built out to it. You need the railroad for shipping out and for bringing in equipment. Either the Arizona & New Mexico line or the Southern Pacific would want a big share. We might bid them against each other, but the nearest smelter is in Silver City and only the Southern Pacific goes up there. Then, you got to hire miners and overseers and assayers and geologists."

"Does Don Emilio have a railroad?"

"Don't need one," said Cody.

"Doesn't," said Lisa-Marie. "He *doesn't* need one."

"Look," said Cody with irritation, "quit correcting me like some old-maid schoolmarm."

"Old maid! I'll show you who's an—"

"Cut it out," said Noel impatiently. "What does he use instead?"

"Wagons. Don Emilio's got peons and Indians working like slaves for him. Leastways, that's what Uncle Frank says. And he's got enough vaqueros to guard his wagon shipments. We ain't set up for no big operation like that. Grandpa says it's more headache than it's worth and that we ought to stick with cows, which is a business we know."

"But if your grandfather brought in investors," began Noel thoughtfully, "he could—"

"Nope!" said Cody. "The Double T stays in the family. No outsiders."

Noel thought it was a shortsighted stance, considering the wealth the family could accrue if they developed their mineral holdings, but it wasn't his business. At least now he understood why the little ranch was so valuable.

He drew a deep breath. "What's the layout of this place,

and what's the best way out?"

Before anyone could answer, a knock on the door preceded Don Emilio's entrance. Cody turned bright red, and Lisa-Marie resumed her big-eyed look of adoration for Noel. By now he'd figured out that most of her seeming infatuation with him was just an act to put Don Emilio off.

"Ah," said Don Emilio, raising his brows. "So this is where you have disappeared to. I thought I said Señor Kedran should not have visitors until tomorrow."

"I was just seeing to his dinner tray," said Lisa-Marie, batting her lashes. "A hero has to have sustenance."

"And I just came by to thank him for rescuing my sister," said Cody, stammering over his words. "We weren't doing anything wrong."

"No, of course not," said Don Emilio, his hazel gaze moving watchfully to each of their faces. "But Señor Kedran needs his rest. You must not tire him."

Apologizing, both of the twins headed reluctantly for the door. Lisa-Marie glanced over her shoulder with a look of entreaty. Fortunately Don Emilio misunderstood it.

"Naughty, *muchacha*," he said with a smile and shook his finger at her. "These looks of passion will bring back his fever, I think. Tomorrow you will speak to him only in the drawing room, as is proper. And you will have your brother or Señora Chavez to chaperone you."

Lisa-Marie stared at him in outrage. "That's gothic! Noel is a perfect gentleman."

"Perfect gentlemen do not entertain young ladies in their bedchambers while they are half-dressed."

"But he's sick."

"He has been, but he is no longer. You will have a *dueña*. Now off to bed, both of you."

"Good night, Noel," they chorused. This time both of them sent him looks of appeal. He wondered why they weren't

SHOWDOWN

more obvious about it. Why didn't they cross their eyes at him or make cryptic gestures? They might as well shout in front of Don Emilio, who was bound to get suspicious if they kept this up.

"Night," Noel said shortly and scowled at them.

"Oh, one last thing," said Don Emilio. "The messenger I sent to the Double T has returned."

They turned to him eagerly. "How's Uncle Frank?" said Cody.

"I regret that your uncle is dead."

Their eyes widened. Both turned pale and stricken. Lisa-Marie put her fingers to her mouth and wept.

"I am sorry," said Don Emilio, and his rich voice was soft with compassion. "There was no kind way to tell you this terrible news. My men are still hunting the Comancheros. You can be sure they will find them. These outlaws will pay."

Cody put his arm around his weeping sister and faced Don Emilio. "We'd like to go home for the funeral."

"Of course. However, your grandfather is on his way to fetch you. He will be here late tomorrow. Now go to bed and say your prayers for the soul of your uncle. *Buenas noches.*"

When they were gone, Don Emilio turned to stare at Noel. Their eyes held for a long, long time. Steel lay at the back of Don Emilio's gaze.

"They fear me, these children, because of the long enmity between my father and their grandfather. You are a good man, Noel. I like you very much. But I warn you now, do not interfere."

Trying to look innocent and noncommittal, Noel said nothing. Don Emilio left without another word.

As soon as he was alone, Noel activated his LOC.

"Data retrieval, you useless pile of junk," he said. "Make

it fast, and it had better be accurate. Tell me about the silver deposits on the Double T."

Humming, the LOC said, "Initially silver mining in New Mexico territory was centered in Magdalena and Socorro in mid-nineteenth century. By the early part of twentieth century, Silver City had surpassed other mining centers."

"Great," muttered Noel, his patience running thin, "but that isn't what I asked for. Specifically I want to know about silver deposits on the Double T."

The LOC remained silent.

"Are you malfunctioning?" asked Noel.

"Negative. Anomaly warning. Parallel history."

"Aha!" said Noel. "Tell me about each of the parallels. Quickly!"

"Original history: Lisa-Marie Navarres inherited Double T from Frank Trask. Her husband, Don Emilio Navarres, opened extensive mining production, with gross profits in excess of $500,000 yearly."

"My God," said Noel in astonishment. "Half a million dollars? Silver was never that lucrative."

"Silver is frequently a by-product of copper mining. After 1905, copper production bypassed that of silver and gold. Navarres was able to produce copper, silver, zinc, and lead from deposits discovered on the Double T. In 1942, Esteban Navarres sold the mining rights to Federated Mining, Inc. In 1960, a revised survey in search of vanadium deposits turned up carnotite—one of the main mineral sources of vanadium and uranium. The discovery of uranium ore in the southwest region of the state revived mining operations there. Previously, uranium deposits in New Mexico had been found primarily in the San Juan Basin. By 1994, this was the largest source of uranium in the United States. Production—"

"Stop." said Noel. "What's the parallel?"

"Anomaly warning."

"Yes, yes, I know there's an anomaly. Go on."

"Parallel one: Lisa-Marie Trask inherits the Double T from Thomas Trask as the sole survivor of the family. In 1890 she marries Don Emilio Navarres—"

"Stop. What's the next parallel?"

"Parallel two: Cody Trask inherits the Double T in 1889. No mining operations are conducted. In 1936, his daughter Rebeccah Trask inherits the ranch. In 1938, she sells it to Horton Avery of Roswell. Avery and his family run cattle on the land until 1957 when a drought puts them out of business. The state leases expire, and—"

"Stop," said Noel. "Question: Is uranium discovered on the property?"

"Negative. The southwest region of the state is never developed. Dr. Samuel Corto's experiments with the Stanheid Fission Accelerator fail due to lack of sufficient uranium supplies. The—"

"Wait a minute," broke in Noel anxiously. "Corto was the leading physics genius of the late twenty-first century. His work with isotopes was ultimately a dead end, but some of his quantum theories were used by Sanders and—and by Korbachevsky to discover the Time Dynamics Principles. Corto was the great-great-grandfather of time travel. Are you saying that without the uranium on this little cattle ranch, time travel is never invented?"

The LOC hummed a moment. "Affirmative."

Noel's knees lost their strength. He sank down on the edge of his bed, feeling stunned as though someone had socked all the breath from him.

"Any more parallels?" he asked weakly.

"Negative. Parallel two is increasing. Parallel one and original history are decreasing."

"How much time do I have left before the safety-chain programming yanks me out of here?"

"Maximum remaining time forty-eight hours, six minutes, eighteen seconds."

Noel bent over until his elbows rested on his knees. He ignored the pain in his back, and thought he had never faced such a terrible choice in his life. "Unless Cody Trask dies in the next two days," he said aloud, "time travel ceases to exist. Then what happens to me? What happens to all the other travelers out there in their respective time streams?"

"Unknown," said the LOC.

"I wasn't asking you," he snapped.

"Affirmative."

Noel sighed. "I caused this. I changed history. Dammit, I like that boy! I don't want him to die."

The LOC remained silent.

It was like a nightmare he couldn't escape. Noel rubbed his face. His head was throbbing. He knew the temptation to lie down and pull the covers over his head. The candles burning by his bed were guttering, white wax bubbling and pooling over the base of the silver candlesticks. Long shadows stretched across the room. He thought of Cody and Lisa-Marie, tucked away somewhere in this silent house, waiting in the night for him to come and lead them to safety.

I have to lead that boy to his death, he thought, and everything in him protested.

"How does Cody die?" he asked. "LOC, respond."

"Unknown."

"I won't kill him myself," said Noel fiercely. "I saved his life. I won't take it."

"Is that a rhetorical—"

"No, it's not!" He heard his voice getting shrill and fought to calm himself down. "There have to be alternatives. Maybe I can persuade Cody to open a mine. The end result would be the same, right?"

"Probability factor is—"

"Don't give me the odds," said Noel. "Scan this house and tell me where Cody and Lisa-Marie are. I've got a breakout to plan."

CHAPTER 13

The hacienda Navarres was laid out in a large U shape surrounding a courtyard filled with a splashing fountain, small willow trees, roses, bougainvillea, and jasmine. The adobe walls were four feet thick and stuccoed. Most of the windows were tiny, but the interior of the house remained cool and comfortable no matter how hot the temperatures climbed outside. Beyond the house stood extensive stables housing the don's prized collection of Arabian and Barbary horses imported from Spain as well as the remuda of sturdy mustangs used by his vaqueros to work cattle. In addition there were various other outbuildings, including the bunkhouses and servants quarters. The whole of this compound was enclosed by a tall adobe and plaster fence perhaps six feet high and thick enough to stop any bullets or arrows from marauding Apaches. Sentries walked the top of the fence by day. At night, they kept themselves hidden at the corners of the walls, crouched to present a lesser target in the moonlight. Another sentry was always in place on top of the windmill tower as well.

The place was a fortress, practically a town. Nearly a

hundred people lived inside the compound, and the nearest village was five miles due west. The U.S.-Mexican border lay nearly a day's ride north, and the Double T was maybe another ten or fifteen miles beyond it.

Using the LOC's electromagnetic damping field, Noel was able to skulk through the hacienda's rambling corridors and loggias without detection by the few sleepy servants still up and around. Most of the house lay shrouded in dark silence. Reaching Cody's room was a simple matter.

Noel crept stealthily inside and let his eyes adjust to the room's shadows. Cody slept on a narrow bed with the sheet in a wild tangle and one foot thrust out through the slats of the painted iron footboard. The window was open to let in the night air, and a cat crouched on the deep sill.

It hissed at Noel and sprang away. Cody never stirred. Noel advanced to his side and stood gazing down at him. The boy slept with deathlike quietness, the way young children sleep, their very innocence freeing them from the restless, worried slumbers of adulthood. Cody looked cramped as though the bed was too small for him. His head was burrowed half beneath the pillow. His chest barely rose and fell with each slow, steady breath.

Do it now, whispered a voice in Noel's mind.

His hands curled into fists and he stepped back, horrified at himself and by how easy it would be. The choice curled before him like a rattlesnake: survival or murder.

That was the way Leon thought. Noel grimaced, wondering if part of Leon hadn't tainted him during that brief joining in the time stream. Leon would not hesitate to eliminate the boy if he deemed it necessary. How ironic that this time the tampering with history was not Leon's fault.

Noel bent over Cody and placed his palm across the boy's mouth.

Cody awakened with a start.

"Hush," whispered Noel. "It's me."

The whites of Cody's eyes glimmered pale in the shadows. "Noel," he whispered back, his lips tickling Noel's palm. Noel dropped his hand away. "Golly, I thought you were never coming. Have you got Lisa-Marie?"

"No. Get dressed."

The boy didn't waste any time. He jerked his pants and boots on, then stuffed his shirttails in with his shirt still unbuttoned. Picking up his hat, he gave Noel a nod. The whole process took maybe two minutes.

Noel admired his quick readiness to action, supposing it was a quality necessary for survival in this land. Hair-trigger reactions, no artifice, no self-delusions, and a clear sense of right and wrong were all characteristics vital for a westerner. Come to think of it, Noel mused, those characteristics would serve anyone just about anywhere. They were qualities desperately needed in his own time, where people preferred to live in dream states supplied by chips in their heads, letting others make their decisions, letting machines and technology do all the work for them, letting their lives slide by unnoticed while they sought something better.

Together, Noel and Cody made their way into the grander portion of the hacienda, where the drawing rooms, dining room, music room, and library were located. A beautifully carved staircase rose to the upper story. Now they had to be cautious indeed. The family bedchambers were located upstairs, Don Emilio's included.

At the top of the stairs, Cody caught Noel's arm. "She's down at the far end," he whispered. "Señora Chavez sleeps in her room."

"Hell," breathed Noel. "This is worse than the Middle Ages."

"Maybe we should try the window."

SHOWDOWN

Noel looked at Cody through the darkness. He wondered if the boy had any idea of what climbing to an upstairs window entailed. Thorny vines, rotten trellises, insufficient toeholds, the threat of breaking your neck, not to mention the possibility of getting the wrong room altogether.

"Stay here," he whispered and moved stealthily down the hallway to Lisa-Marie's door. It was flanked on either side by heavy Spanish chairs covered in red brocade. The door itself was constructed of thick wood planks bound with strap iron. The lock held firm.

Noel turned his back to Cody, still waiting near the staircase, although in the dim light he doubted the boy could see anything. "LOC," he whispered, "retain disguise mode, but extend electrical field and loosen the door hinges."

The LOC grew warm on his wrist. A few seconds passed, then the top hinge creaked alarmingly and shattered. Metal shards whizzed dangerously past Noel, who ducked just in time. From inside Lisa-Marie's room, he heard a woman's voice raised in frightened inquiry.

Swearing beneath his breath, Noel whirled from the door and ran down the hallway. He was even with Don Emilio's door when Señora Chavez wrenched hers open.

"Thief! Seducer! Bandit!" she screeched. "Help!"

Don Emilio's door opened, and Noel bolted past Cody to the stairs. He missed the top step and went down the rest off balance, feet skidding and arms flailing. At the bottom, Noel lost his balance completely and fell on his hands and knees. The jolt made him swear, but Cody leapt past him at a run, his boots clumping on the tiled floor.

"Come on!" he called.

Noel scrambled to his feet, feeling as though his knees were broken. He tangled himself promptly in a rug lying at the foot of the stairs and went sprawling again, catching himself on his scraped palms.

A bullet whizzed over his head, followed by Don Emilio's furious shout.

"Santa Maria! Are you mad? You will kill everyone in the house, shooting in the dark like that."

Lantern light flared down the staircase. Noel righted himself and glanced back just in time to see Don Emilio wrench a pistol from the hand of a servant. Noel ran for it, feeling like a rabbit caught in a maze.

He caught up with Cody in the library, a dead end. Cody crouched by a massive mahogany desk, digging through the drawers with a desperation that left the contents strewn ruthlessly.

Noel said, "What in blazes are you doing?"

"Got to get me a gun," said Cody. "I'm gonna take Lisa-Marie out of here, and if they're shooting, I'm shooting back."

Noel grabbed his arm and yanked him up. Cody still had hold of the drawer, and it flew out of the desk, scattering papers in all directions. "Don't be a fool!" said Noel. "No one's going to shoot."

"They done started it," said Cody grimly.

"We don't have time to argue now. We've got to get out of here. Come this way—"

"No!" cried Cody, twisting free. "I ain't leaving without my sister."

"We can't help her if they catch us. Come on!"

Noel pushed him back toward the music room, where tall French windows overlooked the gardens in the courtyard. Noel barked his shin in the darkness on the sharp corner of a low table and swore furiously, limping the rest of the way to the windows.

"Get these open," he panted.

Together, they pushed their way outside into the lush greenery, a startling oasis of leaf and blossom created in this sere climate. Noel blundered through a thorny rosebush, snagging his clothing and sending crimson petals cascading to the ground. A startled bird flew from the willow tree.

Inside the house, he heard voices raised in commotion. Candles and lanterns were lit, spreading light through the windows into the garden.

"Keep to cover," whispered Noel. "Where's her window?"

"You going to double back?" asked Cody excitedly. "With nerves like that, no wonder you could take on the 'paches."

"Yeah, I'm so great I scare myself," muttered Noel.

Crouching low, they scurried from bush to bush, trampling flowers and low shrubs. The perfumed fragrances of jasmine and gardenia cloyed the air.

Cody snagged Noel's sleeve and pointed skyward. "Up there. See where the light's shining?"

"Oh, great," said Noel. He glanced back across the courtyard to the point where they'd exited. Although they'd closed the French doors behind them, someone would soon think to search out here. They had very little time.

"I'll climb up there—"

"No," said Noel. "I'll do it. Do you know which way the stables are from here?"

"Yeah, but how can we steal horses now with everyone on the warpath?"

"No problem," said Noel, refusing to admit he hadn't thought of a solution yet. "You keep watch and give me a signal if anyone comes this way."

Hoping the quiet splash of the fountain would mask the noise he made, Noel scrambled up the nearest post of the loggia that bordered the courtyard and managed to hoist himself onto its sloped roof. A clay tile came loose and skittered off the edge, shattering with a shrill ring that brought the voices this way.

It was pointless to swear. Noel dashed the sweat from his

eyes and started crawling up the crumbling stuccoed wall toward the window. He was halfway to it when a soft owl hoot from below caught his attention.

Panting, his cuts stinging from sweat, Noel braced his boot toe on a support beam projecting from the wall and glanced down. He saw Cody and Lisa-Marie standing side by side, both staring up at him. Annoyance stung him, and suddenly he felt like a fool.

"What are you doing down there?" he called softly.

"I climbed out the window as soon as Señora Chavez locked me in," said Lisa-Marie. "Come on down."

Why hadn't she shown up sooner? He choked back the temptation to yell at her and gestured furiously. "Get to the stables. I'll join you there."

They hesitated a moment, then Cody tapped his sister on the shoulder and they melted into the shadows. Seconds later, while Noel was still trying to figure out how to maneuver himself down, Don Emilio and a handful of servants burst into the courtyard and fanned out.

Don Emilio's distinctive voice was not smooth now. It was iron-hard, issuing orders in rapid Spanish. Noel resisted the instinctive urge to plaster himself to the wall and instead scurried upward as fast as he could. He caught the window ledge, dangled precariously for a few moments until his scrambling feet found toeholds, and dragged himself bodily inside the room.

Sprawling on the floor, he rested for a moment to regain his breath. His chest and back throbbed mercilessly, and he thought that heroism was for the birds.

As a guest room, Lisa-Marie's lacked a great deal. It was tiny, barely large enough to hold a narrow bed of heavily carved walnut, a night table, a crucifix, and an armoire. The door stood open, and beyond it could be glimpsed a larger chamber filled with candlelight.

SHOWDOWN

Noel was picking himself up when he heard a scolding voice coming. A woman dressed in a voluminous, ruffled wrapper and shawl stepped inside. She froze at the sight of him. Her small plump hands went to her mouth, and her eyes widened until he thought they might pop.

"Sangre de Cristo," she said, most improperly, and seized an unlit candlestick from the bedside table. She rushed at him, brandishing the candlestick like a wild woman. "Thief! Brigand! Rapist! Murderer! You steal my Lisa-Marie, my *niña del ojo*. You wicked man! You beast! You—"

Ducking beneath the rain of blows, most of which were as glancing as they were inaccurate, Noel seized her wrist and wrenched the candlestick from her hand. She sputtered and struggled, but beneath her plump form lay no real strength.

"Oh!" she cried. "Oh, *Dios!*"

She swooned suddenly, making herself an unwieldy, limp burden of incredible weight. Puffing, Noel struggled with her and managed to drag her to Lisa-Marie's unslept-in bed. He dropped her upon the snowy expanse of starched linen trimmed with Battenberg lace and dashed through the larger room to the door. Just as he eased it open, however, a trio of servants appeared in the corridor.

They gave a shout. "There he is!"

Cursing, Noel bolted down the length of the corridor with them chasing right on his heels. One of them tried to tackle him, but Noel twisted with a burst of desperate speed. The man's fingers clutched at the back of his shirt and lost their hold. Noel ran faster, not daring to glance back.

The corridor dead-ended. Skidding to a halt on the polished floor, his feet tangling in a rug woven of bright colors, Noel could not stop his impetus and slammed into the wall with his shoulder. The men shouted eagerly, but there was a wooden ladder attached to the wall. Without hesitation Noel scrambled up it, and burst through the trapdoor in the roof.

He wriggled his way into the soft night air and dropped the trapdoor closed on his pursuers. A wail muffled beneath the wood told him that at least one had fallen off the ladder. He wasted precious seconds with the iron ring bolt, seeking a way to lock the door, and found nothing.

Giving up, he fled across the flat rooftop, crouching low to keep his silhouette from showing above the short wall bordering the roof's edge. He paused only once, panting hard, to take his bearings. There were covered walkways between the separate buildings on this side of the compound. If he stayed on the roof, he could go almost the entire way to the stables.

Behind him, the trapdoor crashed open. He heard curses and furious expostulations from his pursuers. Noel glanced back and saw three figures silhouetted in the moonlight. He crouched low in the shadows and scuttled along the wall to the end of the roof. Then, with one quick bound, he vaulted the wall and hit the sloping roof tiles of hard-baked clay. His heels skidded, dislodging tiles that shattered loudly on the ground below. Men searching the courtyard looked up. There were more shouts.

Noel flailed his arms to keep his balance. He couldn't slow down; he was sliding too fast. He crouched, trying not to look at the ground below, and jumped the distance between the edge of this overhang and the next section of roof.

He landed badly, banging his knees and sending more roof tiles shattering. They slid under his hands and feet, granting him little purchase as he struggled to climb up the overhang to the low wall. Finally he managed to grab a splintery support beam. He clutched it just as both feet slid out from under him and he landed hard on his hip. Gasping for air, he pulled himself up and balanced precariously on the support beam before climbing up and over the wall bordering this new section of roof.

SHOWDOWN

The next jump was easier. No overhangs this time to maneuver, and he made the leap to the flat top of the stables without difficulty. But his pursuers had anticipated him. He saw a group of them ringing the stables. The horses in the corrals milled about, slinging their heads and nickering nervously.

It was the last building of the row. Noel wiped his face with his sleeve and crawled about in search of a trapdoor.

There was none.

"Get him!" shouted a voice.

He heard the slap of a ladder against one wall, but before he could react Cody whooped loudly. Horses, already frightened by the commotion, suddenly plunged out an open gate in the corral. Noel glimpsed Cody and Lisa-Marie riding in their midst, crouched low behind flying manes.

The men yelled after them, shouting for the sentries to stop them at the main gates.

He started down, but from the corner of his eye he glimpsed a shadow climbing onto the roof. The man rushed at him, and Noel turned just in time to grapple with him. They rolled, gouging and slamming fists into each other. Each blow to Noel's welts reawakened the old agony. Knowing he could not last long, Noel clipped the man with a dirty blow. His opponent gave a hoarse, gargling cry and slumped. Noel squirmed free and saw another climbing onto the roof.

Yelling, Noel rushed forward and pushed the ladder away from the stables. The men on it screamed, and the ladder swayed a moment before toppling backward to the ground. Men jumped frantically from it in all directions, like fleas jumping off a wet dog. Grinning to himself, Noel took a running start and jumped the distance between the stables and the compound wall.

He was tired, and he misjudged the distance. He landed short, his toe slipping off the flat top of the wall and bringing him down hard across it. He wheezed, consumed with agony, and gripped the rough plastered surface with desperate fingers.

A hand closed around his ankle. Noel managed to kick free. He pitched himself headfirst over the wall, his impetus flipping him in midair so that he landed flat on his back in the middle of a mesquite thicket.

Thorns ripped through his clothing and skin. He howled in pain and thrashed to get free. By the time he succeeded, blood ran freely from the scratches. He staggered around in a small circle, trying to regain his wits as well as his bearings.

From atop the wall a sentry shouted something in rapid Spanish. There came the almost simultaneous crack of a rifle, and a bullet thudded into the sand a scant foot from Noel. He dived to the ground and squirmed into the shadows at the base of the wall, his heart going like thunder inside his sore ribs. Maybe he shouldn't have listened to the kids. Maybe he should have trusted Don Emilio and stayed put in that big comfortable bed where he belonged.

Now he was out, although he might have a hole in his hide at any minute, but the twins were still inside the compound. They were mounted, but they couldn't get through the gates unless he did something.

Noel crawled along rapidly, his elbows digging hard into the abrasive sand. Now and then he encountered a thorny branch of mesquite lying on the ground like a booby trap.

When he thought he was safely past the sentry, he got cautiously to his feet, still hugging the wall and the deep shadows at its base, and trotted along as fast as he could.

And all the while, a little voice was yammering in the back of his head, telling him to give up this foolishness, to let Don Emilio hold the twins for ransom if he wished, to let Don Emilio marry the girl and eliminate the boy, to let Don Emilio take ownership of the Double T and develop it. Otherwise, all

Noel was accomplishing tonight was to seal the altered events of history and thereby destroy his own future.

"LOC," he said softly, urgently. "Project electrical field to main compound gates. Are you within range?"

"Affirmative," intoned the flat voice of his wrist computer.

"Loosen all hinges and locks," said Noel. "Do it *now*!"

"Affirmative," said the LOC. "Accomplished."

Ahead, around the corner of the wall, Noel could hear an outcry go up and the sound of rapid hoofbeats. His head came up. Were they through the gates? Were they free?

No sentry guarded the corner. With the birds flown, what was the point? Panting, his legs burning, Noel pushed himself into a run and dared break cover into the moonlight.

Moments later he heard hoofbeats approaching and saw two horses coming his way. The moonlight shone bright on Lisa-Marie's hair. Noel stumbled to a halt, and they reined up on either side of him.

"Get up behind me," said Cody, jerking his foot free of the left stirrup and reaching down his hand.

Noel swung up behind the boy and gripped close, feeling the boy's muscles ripple in his back. Cody wheeled the snorting horse around and kicked it to a gallop. Beside them, Lisa-Marie kept even, her hair streaming behind her, the horse's mane whipping across her hands.

They rode flat out for perhaps five hundred yards, then Noel heard the ground rumble. He glanced at the star-spangled sky for storm clouds, but even as he looked he knew it wasn't thunder he heard. Behind them came a horde of riders, swarming upon them, overtaking them with whoops and laughter. They circled until the runaways' mounts slowed and finally stumbled to a halt. Perhaps twenty vaqueros surrounded them, laughing and swinging coiled lariats in their hands.

"Break for it again!" they called. "Give us a real chase. Let us rope you like maverick steers, eh?"

"Let us go!" shouted Lisa-Marie, her voice raw. "You have no right to keep us against our—"

"Right?" interrupted a deep voice. It rolled out through the darkness, and the jeering vaqueros abruptly hushed. Their ranks parted, and Don Emilio came riding up on his fine stallion. The horse pranced and snorted, tossing its beautiful head. Hatless, his white shirtfront a pale blur in the shadows, Don Emilio's anger was strong enough to be felt.

Noel tensed and dropped his hold around Cody. He wanted to be ready for anything.

"Is it *right* for you to disrupt my entire household in this bizarre manner?" demanded Don Emilio. "Is it *right* for you to sneak from my house in the dead of night like thieves?"

"We had no choice," retorted Lisa-Marie. "You were keeping us prisoner—"

"A strong word," he interrupted. "And a stronger misconception. I am not your enemy, *muchacha*."

"Then why wouldn't you let us go home? Why bring Grandpa here unless you intend to force him to give you his ranch?"

"Yeah," put in Cody.

Don Emilio said nothing for a moment. His horse tossed its head and pranced restively. "Noel?" he said at last, and his voice held disappointment. "You have assisted them in this mad delusion. I thought you were a man of sense."

"They want to go home," said Noel carefully, trying to gauge the extent of Don Emilio's anger. "Why not let them?"

"Not this way," said the Mexican. "Not with the Apaches stirred up and outlaws running free. Not alone. Not at night. Señor Trask will arrive tomorrow, and we will talk. It is the way—"

"You know good and well Grandpa won't give you the

time of day unless he's forced to," said Cody furiously. "You're just trying to force him—"

"No one is being forced to do anything!" shouted Don Emilio. "Santa Maria, how many times must I say it?"

"Then let us go home," said Lisa-Marie. "Prove your honor by releasing us."

Before Don Emilio could reply a rider came galloping out of the brush. He reined up so violently his horse reared. "Don Emilio! Quickly—"

"Yes?" said Don Emilio. "Who are you?"

"Pedro Rodriguez, señor."

"Ah, *bueno*," said Don Emilio. "You have brought the old man more quickly than I expected—"

"No, no, señor. I beg your pardon a thousand times, but I must give you bad news. He is gone."

Lisa-Marie gave a choked cry. "Grandpa?"

"Explain," said Don Emilio swiftly.

"The Comancheros attacked us just as we stopped to camp for the night. They killed Luis and Tomas, and rode off with him. Agustine is badly hurt, a bullet in the chest. I rode here as fast as I could."

"No," said Cody. "No! We've got to go after them. We've got to—"

Noel touched his shoulder. "Easy, Cody. Don't go off half-cocked."

Cody shrugged off his hand. "I'm going now—"

Don Emilio spurred his horse forward to block Cody's. "Don't be a fool! We must think. We must plan."

"This ain't none of your—"

"Of course it is! Now accept my help and do not make me more angry with you than I already am." Don Emilio gestured to his men. "Pedro, go on to the hacienda and get a fresh horse and canteens. Catch up with us. Can we be at your camp before dawn?"

"*Sí*, señor."

"*Bueno*. Do you know which direction they were heading? You had better tell Miquel I want him for a tracker."

"Señor, they said that if you wanted El Raton you must go to Silver Canyon."

Noel's ears pricked up at that.

Don Emilio snorted. "*Dios*, he is setting a trap for me. He will regret it."

Cody and Lisa-Marie exchanged looks through the darkness. For an eerie instant Noel had the impression they were communing.

Cody said, "You'll never find it with a tracker."

"No, this I am aware of. Silver Canyon is a legend. Some do not think it exists, but I know differently. My father saw it once when an old Indian took him there as a boy. He was blindfolded going in and out, and could not find it again. It would seem El Raton has been more fortunate than I."

"We know where it is," said Cody.

Don Emilio drew a sharp breath of air. "That is what I thought," he said softly.

"But we're not going to tell you," said Lisa-Marie. "Never."

"You have no choice," said Don Emilio. "Your grandfather's life is at stake now."

The twins sat in stubborn silence, but Noel could sense Cody's anguish.

"Noel?" said Lisa-Marie, and her voice betrayed her worry.

He frowned at the back of Cody's head and drew a deep breath. "I'm sorry. Don Emilio is right. You need his help, and to get it you will have to pay his price."

"You're as bad as he is!"

"Hush up, Lisa-Marie," said Cody.

"But, Cody—"

"I said to hush up! We've got to do it. We've got no choice." Cody looked at Don Emilio. "You won't need the tracker. I'll show you where the canyon is. Just you make sure nothing happens to my grandpa."

CHAPTER 14

∞

By midmorning the next day, Noel felt like he'd been permanently welded to his saddle. His body ached from the long hours of riding. His eyes stung from lack of sleep. He was hungry and thirsty, and he needed a shave. The sunlight already scorched him. From far away on the western horizon came a flotilla of cumulus clouds, but they looked empty of rain. He inhaled the dry, dusty air and wondered if it ever rained on this desiccated land. He could smell the heat in the gleaming sorrel horsehair on his mount's neck. He could smell the oiled leather of his saddle. He could smell the sharp, unpleasant stench of broomweed crushed by hooves. Ahead on the trail, a rattlesnake loosed a warning. They skirted the coiled serpent, the horses snorting uneasily, and its angry whirring rattle filled the air. A hawk sailed high overhead, oblivious to them.

Cody's horse had a devil's horn around its fetlock. He reined up and dismounted to pull off the barbed seed pod. Noel stopped beside him, letting the others go on.

"How much farther?" asked Noel in a low voice for Cody's ears alone.

"Not far. Maybe a mile. It's in those ridges over yonder." Cody got the devil's horn off and released the horse's foot. It stamped with irritation, and he patted its shoulder. "I'm scared, Noel. They killed Uncle Frank, and I'm scared they're gonna kill Grandpa too. Lisa-Marie still thinks El Raton works for Don Emilio. Do you reckon this is a way to get me to tell him where Silver Canyon is?"

Noel's spirits felt compressed, as though he could sense time running out. He needed to consult his LOC, but there was no privacy. "Maybe," he said cautiously; aware of the keen looks cast his way by the passing vaqueros. "There's still no choice though."

Cody nodded and took off his hat to wipe out the inside. "I know it. I just don't like being outfoxed. And then I reckon what if El Raton is on his own and Don Emilio's all right? It's hard, knowing what's right."

From his saddle, Noel stared down at the bared head of the boy, seeing the straight young shoulders, the deepening chest that spoke of approaching manhood, the spattering of freckles on an honest face. He wanted to tell Cody not to worry, to not try so hard to make the decisions of a man, to stay a boy because today was his last day, and he was perfect as he was.

But he couldn't say any of those things.

Noel glanced up at the sky, squinting against the harsh sunlight that made his eyes water. *Why does he have to die?* But he knew why, and his own reluctance to see it happen was a throbbing force that grew. He had the sudden, wild urge to seize Cody's reins and lead the boy in a gallop to safety, far away from these men and the events that were converging. But he couldn't. Deep inside himself, he was unwilling to lose his own history, his own future, his own place in time—even if he remained trapped forever. He wondered if he was a coward to cling so selfishly to his history. But he knew he could do nothing else. His training and his conscience would not let him alter history, no matter how great the temptation.

"Noel," said Cody, looking up at him with trust and affection, "is something wrong? You crying?"

Noel frowned and looked away hurriedly. "No," he said, blinking. "Got dust in my eyes. Get back on."

Cody mounted, and they caught up with the other riders. Another quarter mile of steady riding, and Don Emilio called a halt. Although his vaqueros scorned carrying canteens as a gringo weakness, Don Emilio helped himself to water and handed his canteen courteously to Lisa-Marie. Then he rode his dusty black stallion back to join Noel and Cody.

"We are across the border," he said.

"Yeah," said Cody. "This is Double T land. The canyon is in those ridges."

Don Emilio frowned. "I have ridden through those ridges many times, and never did I find Silver Canyon."

"They wind around. It's easy to miss the right way in," said Cody.

Don Emilio's hazel eyes narrowed. He looked tired and close to the end of his patience. "Will you show us, so that we can rescue your grandfather quickly, or do you intend to make the old man suffer?"

Cody turned red. "That's not fair. We can't just ride into the canyon. They'd have us, and how could we rescue ourselves, much less him?"

"He has a point," said Noel.

Before Don Emilio could reply, a shout from a vaquero alerted them. A rider was coming at a gallop, dust fogging in his wake. He rode right into their midst before he reined up, and appeared oblivious to the drawn pistols and rifles aimed at him.

Noel stiffened in his saddle and kicked his horse toward the newcomer. "What are *you* doing here?" he demanded.

SHOWDOWN

Leon tipped back his big sombrero and bared his teeth. "You thought you'd gotten rid of me, didn't you, *brother*? Well, you didn't."

Noel glared at him. "Thanks to you, we're stuck here forever."

Leon laughed. "I don't mind. I have friends. And I have wealth." He drew a chunk of ore from his pocket and tossed it on the ground. The sun sparked silver glints from the stone, and the vaqueros gasped.

"Hear me!" said Leon loudly. "I bring a message from El Raton. His men are not in the canyon. Just him and the old man. He wants Cody and Lisa-Marie to come in alone."

Don Emilio drew himself erect, and the sunlight glittered brightly off the silver conchas adorning his fancy saddle. "I have given orders throughout Chihuahua that El Raton is to be brought to justice and hanged. When he was just a petty cattle rustler, I looked the other way. But he goes too far. The price on his head does not come off. And these children do not walk into his trap."

Lisa-Marie glared at Don Emilio. "We aren't children. This is our affair. We didn't ask you for—"

"Hold on," said Cody hastily. "Don Emilio is here to help us out. Don't start insulting him—"

"I'll say what I think," she snapped and turned on Leon. "As for you, if anything happens to our grandfather, El Raton will—"

"Make all the threats you like," said Leon, leering at her in a way that made Noel long to punch him in the mouth. "But if you want the old man back in one piece, you'll do as El Raton says. He wants the kids to come to him."

Don Emilio and Noel exchanged glances. "I am not such a fool," said Don Emilio coldly. "Once he has all the Trasks, he will make demands of me."

"You don't owe us," began Cody, but Don Emilio held up his hand for silence.

"I will talk to El Raton," said Don Emilio.

"Nope," said Leon. "He said if you go in there, he'll blow Trask's head off."

Lisa-Marie cried out, and Cody said grimly, "We'll go."

He spurred his horse forward, but Don Emilio grabbed Cody's reins.

"Turn loose!" said Cody furiously.

"*Dios,* be still!" snapped Don Emilio. "Will you never learn to think before you jump into danger? The man is as wily as the rat he is named for. He cannot be trusted."

"He wants us to let him hide out on our land," said Cody. "You've got him just about run out of Mexico. I aim to agree to what he wants. Later on, we'll get the sheriff to smoke him out."

"That will not work."

Cody looked him in the eye. "It's all I got. Come on, Lisa-Marie. Let's ride."

"I am not letting you enter his clutches alone," said Don Emilio.

Cody took off his hat and slapped it against his leg. "Didn't you hear this hombre? If you ride in with us, El Raton will kill Grandpa. I ain't gonna let that happen."

"Nor will I," said Lisa-Marie.

Don Emilio glared at her. "Did it never occur to you, *muchacha,* that your grandfather could already be dead? Did it never occur to you that I would let the man escape, to rob and pillage again, rather than allow him to harm either of you? If you put yourself in his power, you destroy mine."

Lisa-Marie looked startled. She blinked at Don Emilio, who regarded her like a block of stone. Remote, unreachable, he stared back, the usual compassion absent from his handsome face. Her blue eyes widened and grew dismayed. Watching,

Noel wondered if she had finally realized that Don Emilio had never been her enemy and that she had gone too far with her heedless accusations.

"Noel?" she asked uncertainly.

Don Emilio shot Noel a hard glance. Noel waited for him to speak, but he said nothing.

Noel sighed. "You can't accuse a man of being in league with the bad guys and then expect him to risk his life for you."

Lisa-Marie's face went scarlet. "I don't—I didn't mean it like that. I haven't asked him to do anything for us."

"Sure you have. He keeps holding out his hand in friendship, and you both keep slapping him in the face with an old family feud. He's giving you good advice right now. You know good and well that if you two ride into the canyon alone, we'll have to rescue all of you."

"But we have to save Grandpa!" cried Lisa-Marie.

"You are a child," said Don Emilio, "thinking and reacting impulsively in the way of a child. But even a child may know common civility and courtesy, and depend on them in times of confusion."

"I'm sorry," she whispered, still red-faced. "Please help us."

His nostrils flared. His proud hidalgo look did not melt. For a moment he regarded her in stony silence, then his gaze shifted to Cody. "And you?" he asked curtly. "Do you also think I plotted this abduction with El Raton in order to steal your ranch from you?"

Cody turned as red as his sister. He would not meet Don Emilio's eyes. "Uh, no, sir. But Lisa-Marie is right. No matter how big a mistake it is, we've got to go in after Grandpa. We've got to do it his way. We don't have a choice."

Don Emilio's mouth tightened. His gaze went to Noel, who said quietly, "El Raton's using two kinds of bait, the silver for you and Trask for the twins. Why don't we give him what he wants, but with a little twist?"

"Explain."

Noel looked over at Leon, who was sitting slumped in his saddle, grinning at their argument with one boot heel cocked up on his saddle horn. Noel said to him, "Take off your clothes."

Leon jerked erect and his foot swung down to thump against his horse's side. The animal jumped, but one of the vaqueros had the horse snubbed close. Leon looked around with a snarl.

"No way," he said furiously. "This is none of *your* business, Noel. Don't think you can pull any tricks."

Don Emilio smiled. "You will exchange places with him, no? Ah, Noel, you have a clever mind." He snapped his fingers. "Strip him."

The vaqueros closed in on Leon, who cursed loudly and raked his horse with his spurs. The animal bolted free of the man holding its bridle. Leon lashed it hard with his quirt and galloped away. Noel swore and started to go after him, but Don Emilio flung out his hand.

"Wait, my friend. He won't get far."

Even as Don Emilio spoke, a vaquero galloping flat out behind Leon shook out his lariat and formed a loop. With an easy flick of his wrist, the vaquero threw his rope and caught the hind feet of Leon's horse. He yanked up, swift and hard, and his mount sat back on its hindquarters. Leon's horse was thrown flat to the ground, and Leon went tumbling in a fall that made Noel wince in sympathy.

The other vaqueros caught up, surrounding Leon who was dazedly trying to pick himself up. Dismounting, they shucked him out of his trousers, boots, and shirt. Leon yelled and kicked, but it did him no good. Within seconds he stood there in his socks and long underwear, glowering.

SHOWDOWN

Noel put on Leon's clothes, his skin crawling with repugnance. Everything fit, of course, even the big Mexican sombrero that he jammed on his head. The six-shooter that he buckled on around his hips was surprisingly heavy. When he took the reins of Leon's buckskin, however, Leon came at him.

"Sooner or later you're going to kill Cody," he said, straining against the men who held him back. "Why don't you just draw that pistol and drill him now? Get it over with. Don't be squeamish, Noel. You know all of this is your fault."

Heat flooded Noel's face. He turned away from the furious taunts of his duplicate and mounted swiftly. Leon went on yelling.

"Coward! Yellow-bellied, no-good skunk! Why don't you let them know what you really are? Why don't you tell them how this is your fault and what you're really doing here? Tell them, Noel. You're playing games with their lives. Don't they have a right to understand why? Oh, sanctimonious brother, how they all look up to you. Kill him now, and get it over with. You can't depend on El Raton or one of the others to do it for you."

Frowning, Don Emilio gestured. "Shut him up."

"Tell them the truth, Noel. Tell them—"

A vaquero socked him in the jaw, and Leon sagged unconscious to the ground. There was silence, broken only by the cawing of a flock of ravens. The west wind sighed hot and dry through the greasewood.

Noel closed his eyes, trying to calm the throbbing fury in his veins. He was afraid now if he looked at Cody, the boy would read the truth in his eyes. Damn Leon!

"He is crazy, that one," said Don Emilio flatly. "Loco in the head."

"He sure is," said Cody in wonder. "Why, Noel saved my life. I reckon if anyone wanted to put a bullet in me, it would be Leon. I sure am sorry, Noel, that you've got to put up with a brother like that. He's a shame to you, isn't he?"

Noel's throat was too choked up for him to answer, but he forced himself to meet the boy's trusting gaze. He nodded curtly and wheeled his horse around. "Let's ride."

Don Emilio gave him a small salute. "You are a braver man than I, amigo. Bring them back safe."

They headed up into the low ridges, their mounts scrambling over loose shale. A small herd of perhaps a half-dozen pronghorn antelope sprang from a thicket and flashed over the crest of a ridge in a creamy blur of grace and motion. Blooming pear cactus dotted the hillsides. Lizards and pack rats scurried to cover ahead of them. A covey of fat quail waddled fussily up the trail, then burst into low flight.

Noel glanced back only once, and saw Don Emilio dispersing his men into cover. El Raton's bunch had to be concealed around here somewhere. If anything went wrong, there would be a hot battle of bullets soon. Noel's mouth was dry from more than thirst. He swallowed, but he couldn't work up any spit. There was no canteen on Leon's saddle, and he didn't ask Lisa-Marie to share from hers. El Raton was bound to have his spies watching. Noel reminded himself to act like Leon.

With a wink at Lisa-Marie to warn her, he reached out and fondled her shoulder. "You sure look pretty today," he said loudly and laughed.

"Hey!" said Cody in startlement.

Lisa-Marie shrugged off Noel's hand. "He's just acting like Leon would."

"Yeah?" said Cody, sending Noel a frown. "Well, don't try too hard."

Noel couldn't tell if Cody was seriously annoyed or acting. Maybe Leon's parting words were gnawing at him. He glanced frequently at Noel, his eyes holding a frown. As for himself, Noel couldn't shake Leon's words either. Time was running out. He guessed he had been hoping an accident would befall the boy, but Leon was right about that being a cowardly hope. Noel was ashamed of himself for even thinking that way.

Yet he couldn't commit cold-blooded murder. The very thought of doing so made his head go light. He swallowed hard, sweating in the heat and glare, and knew the act was not in him. Even if history changed and time travel was never invented, even if he had to spend the rest of his life in this era, even if he ceased to exist, he could not draw his pistol and shoot that boy.

"This way," said Cody.

They turned onto a narrow, twisting game trail showing Leon's recent tracks and headed up a steep slope. At the crest Noel saw nothing but rock and round cedar bushes—a broken, jumbled country that betrayed no secrets. Rounded boulders, some of them the size of houses, lay stacked in fantastic geological formations. Slabs formed natural lintels across narrow gaps. Immense fingers of rock jutted toward the sky. It was a rock climber's dream. It would be a lost man's nightmare. In the distance, a bobcat stood atop an outcropping, lapping water from a natural indentation in the rock. It snarled at them, and sprang away.

"Go straight down the trail about twenty feet to those big rocks, then go through them," said Cody. "Do you remember the way, Lisa-Marie?"

She was gazing around her in a kind of exaltation, no doubt remembering other, happier times. "Yes, I'm beginning to. It's been so long since we played here."

"How," said Noel, "do I go through rocks?"

"You'll see," said Cody with a grin. "Go on."

The boulders were taller than Noel on horseback. At first they seemed to be solidly against each other, but when he reached them he found a narrow crack separating them. The gap was choked with cedar and brush. It looked like a gloomy hole, and Noel was conscious of the bobcat and possibly its larger cousins—mountain lions—that could be lurking, ready to pounce. His horse snorted and stopped.

"We can't go through there," said Noel.

"Yes, you can. It don't look—"

"Doesn't," said Lisa-Marie. "It *doesn't*."

Cody scowled at her. "It *don't* look like there's room, but just you start. The horse'll fit. Watch your knees, though."

Doubtful, Noel urged his mount forward. After some head slinging, the animal went willingly enough. Scraped by cedar boughs that nearly dislodged his hat, Noel had to take his feet from the stirrups and draw his knees up to protect them. The flapping stirrups knocked and scraped against rock on either side. The trail plunged down steeply, causing the horse to lurch and pick its way with slow caution. But after a few moments, the ground abruptly leveled, and they emerged from the claustrophobic pass into a deep canyon with steep sides of stone rising straight up to the sky.

Lisa-Marie emerged behind him, and gave a low laugh of wonder that echoed off the cliffs. "I'd forgotten how special it is. Just look, Noel!"

"Quiet," said Cody, crowding her from behind. "Don't give us away now."

Subdued at once, she nodded. But she was right. It was a magical place. In the distance could be heard the sound of rushing water. A stream as clear as crystal burbled over a stony bed in the bottom of the canyon. Grass, startlingly green and soft, spread a lush carpet over the ground, and full-sized cottonwood and willow trees cast dappled shade that looked inviting. The air was cool and invigorating. Noel inhaled deeply.

"I never dreamed a place like this could exist here in the desert," he said. "It's like an oasis."

"There's a waterfall farther on," said Lisa-Marie. "You can hear it."

Instead of water, he heard a horse nicker. Noel tensed, and drew his pistol. "We can't enjoy nature now. Ride ahead of me."

Cody took the lead, his face taut and serious beneath the brim of his hat. Lisa-Marie rode next in line, and Noel brought up the rear. Their horses' feet made little sound on the soft grass. Noel's mount put down his head to eat, and Noel kicked him to keep him going.

Beyond the trees, the canyon ended abruptly with a high, vertical cliff face that boxed it. A narrow waterfall cascaded perhaps forty feet to plunge into the clear pool below. The horses pulled forward eagerly to drink. Noel dismounted, and gestured for the twins to do the same. He looked around, seeking El Raton, and saw no one.

The cliff itself had a precarious trail that wound up to a point halfway to the top. Squinting at it, Noel wondered if there was a cave or some kind of recess behind the waterfall.

"El Raton!" he shouted loudly over the rush of water. His voice echoed back to him. "I have brought them!"

No one appeared. No voice replied. Noel frowned in worry.

"Where *are* they?" asked Lisa-Marie. Her face had grown pale, and her blue eyes shone as though she were fighting back tears.

"El Raton!" shouted Noel. "El Raton, I am here!"

The echoes of his voice faded, and he heard only the cries of birds and the small thunder of the water. The horses munched grass busily.

Noel's sense of uneasiness increased. He didn't like this game. He worried that El Raton had maybe given Leon specific instructions. By failing to follow them now, Noel could be betraying himself. "Where does that trail go?" he asked.

"Up to the silver cave," said Cody. "You reckon he's up there, waiting for us?"

"There's nowhere else."

Cody shook his head. "We ain't got any maneuvering room in there. He'll have us sure."

Noel gestured. "Go on."

Looking frightened, Lisa-Marie started walking, but Cody stood his ground.

"I said we won't have any place to move around in."

"I heard you," said Noel grimly. "Go."

Cody's eyes widened. "Whose side you on, anyway?"

"Yours." Noel gave him a shove just in case El Raton was watching. "Don't be a fool. We started this. We've got to finish it."

"We ought to make him come out."

"He's got the trump card, in case you've forgotten. Cody, don't get stubborn and stupid on me now. Go up the trail."

The boy shook his head, but he went. Single file on the narrow ledge that wound up the cliff, they climbed in silence. In the lead, Lisa-Marie made their progress slow because she had difficulty with her long skirts, having to hold them up with one hand and use the other hand to steady herself. She should have been in the middle, but the ledge was too narrow for one of them to pass her. Noel holstered his pistol to free both hands, and didn't care what El Raton thought.

Although the waterfall wasn't more than two or three feet wide, it cast enough spray for the sunlight to create miniature rainbows. The trail leveled off and widened slightly where it went behind the falls, but the ground was wet and the footing treacherous.

Damp with spray, they edged behind the water and ducked into the small mouth of the cave. For a moment there was only dank darkness around Noel, then he groped his way after the others around a bend, and found himself inside a cavern the size of a spacious room. A tin lantern provided golden illumination, and veins of silver shimmered in the rock walls. At the rear lay a mound of rocks as though left from an old cave-in.

On the floor, wrapped in a blanket, his hat pulled low over his face, lay a man.

"Grandpa!" cried Lisa-Marie, and ran to him. Tenderly she rolled him over. "Grandpa, we're here to rescue you. We—"

She froze a moment, then jerked off the hat. The lantern light fell across a thin, beard-stubbled face. Eyes angry with helplessness glared at them all over a cloth gag.

"Why, Skeet," said Cody in astonishment. "What are you doing here? Where's Grandpa?"

CHAPTER 15

∞

Noel jerked the gag off Skeet. Skeet spat and said urgently, "Trap! You shouldn't ought to have come here. Get out now while you still can."

"But where's Grandpa?" asked Lisa-Marie.

Cody knelt to untie Skeet, but the man shook his head violently. "Never mind about me, boy! Get outta here."

"Not without you," said Cody, struggling with the stubborn knots.

Refusing to join the argument, Noel returned to the mouth of the cave. His heart had quickened with a rush of adrenaline. His senses were on sharp alert. He gripped the Colt .45 in a hand gone sweaty, and eased himself outside to the rear of the waterfall.

The spray dampened his face and shirt, and dripped off the brim of his hat. He held his pistol behind him to protect it from the water and searched the canyon below. The quarry was in the trap, and had taken the bait. How long until El Raton sprang it shut?

A scream from Lisa-Marie made him whirl around, heart hammering, and rush back into the cave. He came up short at the sight of a swarthy, bearded man in a vest and wide leather chaps, holding a Winchester trained on them. Skeet was still tied up on the ground. Cody and Lisa-Marie stood against the rock wall, their hands in the air, their faces tense.

The point of the rifle never shifted from them, but El Raton's dark eyes glanced at Noel. He spat a stream of tobacco juice out between large, yellowed teeth. " 'Bout time you got here, Leon. I told you to hurry."

He spoke in Mexican with a rapid, slurry lisp. The wad of tobacco bulged his right cheek. He shifted the wad with his tongue and jerked his head at Noel. "Tie them up. There's rope in the back of the cave."

In silence Noel obeyed. All this time he'd been expecting El Raton to be hiding in the rocks somewhere at the base of the cliff. But the bandit must have been lurking deeper in the cave. From the entrance, there seemed to be only this one room. However, as Noel reached the back, he saw a low slit in the wall concealed by the tumbled pile of rocks. It must lead to another cavern.

"We came here to make a deal," said Cody. His voice was cracking on him, betraying his fear, but he wasn't backing down. Noel was proud of the boy's courage. "There's no call to tie us up. All we want is our grandpa safe and—"

"Shut up, you stupid brat," said El Raton. "I make no deals with gringos."

"But you said—"

El Raton struck him in the chest with the butt of his rifle, sending the boy staggering against the wall. "Shut up, I said! You are no more important than a flea. She is the one I want."

"Leave me alone!" said Lisa-Marie sharply.

El Raton laughed. "If you are my woman, and your brother and grandfather are dead, señorita, then the Double T is mine.

This silver is mine. Don Emilio's word is law in Chihuahua, but not here north of the border."

He put his arm around her and pulled her close against him, laughing as she struggled and cried out in disgust. "*Si,* I like a fighter."

"Let me go. Let me go!"

Still laughing, he nuzzled her face with his beard; trying to steal a kiss. She bit him, and he jerked back with an oath. "Damn you! Leon! Where is that rope?"

Noel stopped trying to peer through the slitted passageway and snatched up the coil of rope. "Here," he said quickly.

El Raton glared at him. "*Payaso!* Tie them up, *pronto.*"

"I thought you were going to kill them," said Noel.

El Raton's gaze narrowed. He spat, and the tobacco juice narrowly missed Noel's boot toe. "Always you are like a fly in my ear, buzzing and buzzing with suggestions. Do I ask you to tell me what I should do, eh?"

"You won't get away with killin' Tom Trask," said Skeet. "Half the territory'll come after you."

With the rifle still at his hip, El Raton fired point-blank. The report crashed through the cave, deafening everyone and causing rubble to fall from the ceiling. Skeet jerked violently and sprawled back on the ground, his eyes wide open and sightless.

"No!" said Cody in horror. He threw himself at El Raton, who whirled and cocked his rifle.

Lisa-Marie stepped between him and Cody just as he took aim. Frantically, Noel threw himself at El Raton's back, tackling him awkwardly.

The shot crashed out, and the bullet missed both Lisa-Marie and Cody. But when it hit the wall behind them, it ricocheted off the rock with a dangerous ping and nicked Noel in the arm just above his left elbow.

SHOWDOWN

Pain seared him, and El Raton seized on his momentary distraction to twist away. They grappled fiercely, rolling over and over in the dust, and someone's flailing foot knocked over the lantern. Lisa-Marie rescued the light, and Cody hovered over the two fighting men for a chance to help.

El Raton still clung to his rifle with one hand. The other gripped Noel around the throat and squeezed until black dots danced in front of Noel's eyes. He tore at El Raton's face and seized his wrist with both hands, trying to pull that relentless grip away, but El Raton squeezed harder and harder. Noel's lungs burned. He could feel his consciousness slipping, his strength going. His heartbeat was like thunder in his ears. Reaching down, he pulled his pistol from its holster and jammed the muzzle in El Raton's belly. The bandit's dark eyes widened, and his stranglehold eased off.

Cody loomed over El Raton and struck the back of his head with a chunk of rock. El Raton's eyes rolled up. He slumped over Noel. It took Noel a moment to drag in some desperately needed breaths and squirm his way out from beneath the man. Cody dropped the rock and leaned down to give Noel a helping hand.

"Thanks," wheezed Noel hoarsely. He coughed and massaged his aching throat gingerly. A couple more seconds pressure, and his windpipe would have been crushed.

"You think he's got Grandpa stashed back here somewhere?" said Cody, heading for the rear of the cave.

Noel gestured vaguely. "Passageway."

It hurt to talk. He coughed again and sat down, feeling old.

Lisa-Marie picked up the Winchester and held it trained on El Raton. "We ought to put a bullet in him. Killing Skeet in cold blood like that makes him nothing but a murderer. He's lower than a—"

"Better let the courts string him up," said Noel.

He picked up a piece of the rope he'd dropped and used it to tie El Raton's hands behind his back. The bandit was stirring, snorting and making grunts.

Noel looked at him with disgust. "He must have a skull of solid bone."

"If he's hurt my grandpa in any way," said Lisa-Marie in an angry voice, "I'm putting a bullet through him here and now."

"Don Emilio will take care of him for you," said Noel.

She glared at him, and for that instant the young, appealing girl vanished, and a hard-eyed woman of the frontier stood in her place. "It's my right," she said, "to take justice out of his hide myself."

El Raton was conscious now, and listening. His dark eyes darted rapidly, but he said nothing.

Cody's muffled whoop from the next cavern startled them. More dust trickled down from the ceiling. Noel eyed it warily.

"We'd better make less noise in here," he said.

But Cody was emerging, dust-streaked and triumphant, from the passageway. Tom Trask came in his wake. The old man straightened with difficulty, flexing his reddened, rope-burned hands and blinking painfully in the lantern light. Lisa-Marie hurtled into his arms.

"Grandpa!" she cried, her voice choked against his chest. "Oh, Grandpa!"

He hugged her tight. "There now, Lissy. There now. You're all right. There's nothing to cry about."

"I'm not crying," she said with a sniff. "I've been so worried about you."

"Me!" said the old man in astonishment. Slinging an arm around her shoulders, he limped forward. "Why, gal, it's you who got carried off."

Noel took the rifle from her careless hand and gave it to Cody. The boy grinned broadly at him, and Noel smiled back.

Cody held out his hand. "We owe you a lot, Noel Kedran. For a stranger, you've sure been mighty handy."

They shook hard, and Noel couldn't help but think that now history was definitely changed. He touched his LOC briefly, knowing it would no longer operate. Time travel had ceased to exist. He had better start thinking about adapting permanently to this century.

"Poor Skeet," whispered Cody. "He was mighty good to me, and I—"

"Let's get your grandfather and sister down the trail first," said Noel, pulling off his bandanna to tie around his bleeding arm. "Then we'll bury Skeet."

By the time they finished filling in the shallow grave in the soft ground beside the stream, it was well past midday. Dappled sunlight danced over the emerald grass through the leaves of the swaying trees.

Cody straightened up and dusted off his hands. "This is a good place, a place no man should know about or visit. Skeet can rest here. We'll never disturb it."

Trask levered himself to his feet and hobbled over to join them. "I agree, Cody. We should leave the land alone. We take only what we and our livestock need to live. The land can replenish that."

"And the silver?" Noel asked. In his mind, he was thinking, *And the uranium?* "Men have to make progress. Your way of life, sir, won't last forever."

Trask's leathery face did not alter expression. "I know that," he said gruffly. "I've seen white folks come in and settle. I've seen the Apaches driven back time and time again. Geronimo surrendered last fall. There'll never be his like again. I've seen the Mexicans fought back as well. We've taken the whole territory from them. In a few years, New Mexico will join the union as a state. But while I live, nothing on the Double T will change." He cleared his throat. "Hell, though, I'm getting old. I won't be around much longer."

"Sure you will, Grandpa," said Cody.

Noel turned away sharply, unable to listen to more. He walked past the fallen log where El Raton sat with his hands bound behind his back. Lisa-Marie had climbed partway up the short, rock-strewn slope connecting the bottom of the canyon to the steep cliffs. She stood in the sun, heedless of the heat beating down upon her pale skin and reddish-gold hair, and balanced precariously on top of a small boulder.

"Are you going to stay on at the Double T, Noel?" she asked, without glancing at him.

He paused a few feet away from her. "No."

She faced him. "Why not? You're welcome, always."

"Thanks. But I don't belong here. I have to leave."

Her blue eyes were the color of the sky. "Where do you belong then?" she asked. "Are you going back to Chicago?"

He'd thought about it, but her question seemed to clarify something inside him. He shook his head. "No. I can't. It wouldn't be the same as when I left."

"I understand. This canyon's not the same as the last time I came here. The Double T's not the same. Cody's not the same. No one is. Grandpa looks so old to me. He's getting frail, and I used to think he was the strongest man in the world. Cody and I don't think the same way anymore. He wants to live in the past. I've seen Santa Fe and Albuquerque. Some of my friends have been to Europe. They've shown me their sketches and photographs. They talk about things Cody's never heard of. I don't mind that so much, except that he doesn't want to hear about them." She grimaced and shook her head. "I sound stuck-up, don't I?"

"No, you sound grown-up," he said gently. "You're an intelligent woman, Lisa-Marie. Trust yourself, and don't let the men in your family ever stop you from being all you can."

She stared at him in wonder, until Trask called to her. Then she jumped off the rock and ran past him, leaping lightly from stone to stone until she reached the bottom.

"Noel!" called Cody. "Time to go!"

Noel picked his way down the slope. A rattlesnake buzzed a warning from a pile of rocks, and Noel jumped sideways, giving the snake a wide berth. When he rejoined the others, the rattlesnake could still be heard.

"Why didn't you shoot that gentleman?" asked Trask, handing a set of bridle reins to Noel. "This country is crawling with rattlers. I kill every one I come across."

Noel wanted to say there'd been enough killing for one day, but he mounted his horse in silence. El Raton protested that he couldn't get on a horse with his hands tied behind him, but Trask trained the Winchester on him and Cody gave him a boost into the saddle. They had Skeet's horse as an extra mount. Noel led it, and Cody led El Raton's horse.

In single file they rode out of the canyon. They were still picking their way through the gigantic boulders and odd formations when the sound of pitched gunfire opened up in the distance. In the lead, Trask threw up his hand, and they all halted.

"It's got to be Don Emilio fighting El Raton's bunch," said Cody.

"Sí," said El Raton arrogantly. "I told them to wait two hours, then attack. It will not take long to defeat those fancy vaqueros of his."

"What can we do?" asked Noel.

Trask gestured at Cody. "Get up on that ridge yonder and take a look."

Cody went off at a gallop. When he was still below the skyline, he dismounted and threw his reins down to ground tie his mount. Crouching low, he scrambled up the rest of the way, then threw himself belly flat and peered over the crest of the ridge.

"My Comancheros fight like tigers," said El Raton to Noel. "They will send Don Emilio fleeing back to his fancy hacienda with his tail between his legs. Then, before they cut out your miserable tongue, you will explain to them why you dared put ropes upon me."

"Shut up," said Noel tensely.

They waited a few more minutes, listening to the gunfire, then all was silent. Cody sat up and waved his hat wildly before scrambling down the slope to his horse. He came galloping back with a whoop and reined up in a cloud of dust.

"They've got those bandits rounded up and begging for mercy. I saw 'em creeping out from cover with their hands up."

Everyone smiled, except El Raton, who turned pale and silent. They rode down the ridges to the flat, where Don Emilio and his men waited impatiently in the scorching sunshine. The Comancheros who had survived the battle now sat on the ground in a dejected little group, guarded by rifles. Three bodies had been strapped across saddles. A few of the vaqueros were binding up minor wounds.

Don Emilio rose from the slim shade cast by a yucca plant and came forward to greet them with a broad smile. "Señor Trask, I am delighted to see you well."

Trask grunted. "Can't say I feel the same. What are you doing on Double T land?"

"Grandpa!" said Lisa-Marie in rebuke, but her grandfather ignored her.

"That's a straight enough question, isn't it?" said Trask. "I've made it clear before that you're not welcome here."

"Grandpa, stop it," said Lisa-Marie. "Don Emilio and his men helped search for me when the Apaches took me prisoner. He gave Cody, Noel, and I shelter and care. He rode here today to help us rescue you. And now he's put an end to El Raton's bunch once and for all. Don't be rude."

"I'll be as rude as I like," retorted the old man. He faced Don Emilio again, and his expression remained unyielding. "If you did all that for my granddaughter, then thanks. Decent of you. As for El Raton's boys, we'll both profit from being rid of them."

Don Emilio's smile had long since vanished. He inclined his head proudly. *"De nada, señor,"* he said and gestured for his horse to be brought to him. "We shall not detain you. If I may have your prisoner? I think he will find justice swifter and more deserving in Mexico, no?"

"All right," said Trask.

Cody dismounted and took El Raton's reins from Noel. He led the horse forward.

"This is a United States territory," blustered El Raton. "I demand the justice of the gringos."

"You are in a position to demand nothing," said Don Emilio softly. One of the vaqueros led El Raton's horse away.

Noel glanced around the collection of men. Some were still sitting on the ground; others leaned against their horses; a few were mounted. The vaqueros were grinning; they had the cocky, triumphant look of men who had done well and knew it. Leon stood sullenly in Noel's clothes, giving no trouble for once. He was holding his left arm close to the elbow as though it hurt too.

Noel dismounted and walked over to Don Emilio. "A moment please," he said quietly and kept walking so that Don Emilio was obliged to turn his back to the Trasks and keep step with him. "Lisa-Marie—"

"—will never look my way," said Don Emilio grimly, "and her grandfather will never consent to a marriage of alliance. You see how he has ground his own prejudices into the minds of Cody and Lisa-Marie."

Noel frowned in disappointment. "I'm sorry."

Don Emilio shrugged. "Ah, but she is something, is she not? A vision even now, streaked with dirt and her magnificent hair blowing wild in the wind. I have let myself think a little of courting her. There is a fiesta, you see, where the man comes on horseback to the house of the señorita. He carries flowers across his saddle, and he is dressed in his finest *charro* suit. His friends ride with him, and there is a serenade at the young woman's window. Ah, yes, I have thought of it, but thoughts are all I shall ever have. As a matchmaker, Noel, you are not successful."

Noel rubbed the back of his neck, where the sun was scorching it. "I guess that's true. But—"

"Besides, it is you who have caught the señorita's eye."

"Oh, no!" said Noel with a grin. "She was just pretending all that to keep you at arm's length."

"You are kind to say such a thing, but I do not believe you."

"She's not like the Trask men," said Noel. "She's smart and she knows her own mind. The rest is just immaturity, and she's leaving that behind pretty fast. She doesn't agree with their opinions about a lot of things. Mining interests, for one."

Don Emilio's mouth twisted. "You must understand that I promised my father on his deathbed that I would reclaim the mine. It is not a personal obsession, but I like to keep my word. That is all. I have never wanted to maintain the old feud between the Trasks and the Navarres family, but there is pride to be considered. Señor Trask thinks nothing of stepping on mine whenever he has the chance. He is a hard man."

"He's old," said Noel. "Be patient."

"Perhaps." Don Emilio sighed. "If you stay and continue to teach Cody a broader view of the world, then perhaps—"

A sudden commotion broke out. Noel glanced up and saw Leon spring at El Raton's horse. A knife flashed in his hand as he sliced through the bandit's bonds.

"What the devil—" said Noel. He started running toward his duplicate. "Hey! Stop them!"

Several vaqueros started toward Leon, but he was already swinging up behind El Raton, who spurred his horse savagely.

"Damn!"

Without hesitation, Noel jerked the reins of the nearest horse from the hand of its startled owner and climbed on. He kicked it into a gallop, and the animal responded with an explosion of speed.

Only then did Noel realize that he'd borrowed Don Emilio's black Arabian stallion. The animal stretched out its well-shaped head and lengthened its stride, skimming the ground effortlessly. Already they were gaining on the other horse, which labored beneath two riders.

A sound from behind Noel made him glance back. He expected it to be Don Emilio riding after him, but it was Cody, grinning with excitement and lashing his cow pony on both shoulders with the reins.

Noel grinned back, then urged the stallion on. It drew even with El Raton's mount and swerved in so close their stirrups locked. The stallion had obviously been trained for bulldogging, and Noel took the hint. He kicked free of his stirrups and threw himself bodily at Leon and El Raton, using his own impetus to knock them off their horse.

A fall off a galloping horse was a good way to end up with a broken neck. Noel heard the frightened yells of both men as the three of them sailed through the air. His grip had landed on Leon, and he clung desperately to his duplicate until the stunning force of impact with the ground knocked them apart. Noel rolled over several times, scooping dirt into his mouth and flattening several sticker weeds in the process. Every bone felt shaken apart, and he sat up slowly, the world still spinning around him.

Spitting out dirt, he brushed stickers off his shirt and winced as fresh bruises and cuts made themselves felt. To one side of him, El Raton lay in a sprawled heap. He moaned dismally but didn't move.

Cody reined up and jumped off his horse beside Noel. "Golly, that was a tumble! You all right?"

Noel nodded, but before he could speak he glimpsed Leon edging away. Noel lurched to his feet and grabbed Leon by the shirt collar.

"Not so fast," he said. "You've caused enough trouble—"

Leon turned around and swung a roundhouse punch at him. Noel ducked just in time and drove his shoulder into Leon's chest, knocking his duplicate off balance. While Leon was still staggering, Noel got in a series of blows to his stomach, then drove a solid left cross to Leon's jaw that felled the man. Noel's knuckles split painfully. He winced and shook his hand, blowing to take away the sting.

Leon squirmed about in the dust, then pulled himself up. Just in time Noel noticed the glitter of a knife in his hand and dodged a vicious swipe.

"Watch him, Noel!" shouted Cody in encouragement. "Kick his teeth in!"

Leon swung again, and again Noel had to dodge. Leon's pale gray eyes glittered with malevolent intent. "I am going to finish you," he said.

SHOWDOWN

Noel grabbed at Leon's wrist, but Leon twisted free and slashed. The knife blade cut through Noel's shirt but missed skin.

"You finish me, you finish yourself," said Noel breathlessly.

"Not anymore," said Leon with a wild laugh. His thin face, so like Noel's own, glowed with malice. "The time stream is closed. We're here forever. I can exist without you now."

"Don't be so sure," said Noel. "I—"

"Noel!" shouted Cody. "Watch out!"

The warning came too late. El Raton's strong hands seized Noel from behind, pinning his arms and leaving him exposed to Leon's blade. Laughing like a madman, Leon drew back his arm to plunge the knife into Noel, who kicked and struggled frantically, knowing he hadn't a prayer.

"Leon," he said desperately. "Don't—"

Just as Leon swung, a pistol fired. El Raton jerked with a hoarse cry of pain and fell, knocking Noel off balance. Leon's knife blade missed Noel by scant inches. He ducked and scrambled to elude Leon, who was cursing loudly. Leon swung at him again, and Noel threw dirt in his eyes.

Howling, Leon put his free hand to his face and staggered back, giving Noel time to gain his feet. He kicked Leon's feet out from under him, and when Leon fell Noel stamped on his wrist until he dropped the knife. Noel scooped it up.

"Now," he said, panting heavily. "You stay put for a moment."

Leon was still clawing at his face. "You blinded me, damn you!"

Cody ran up beside Noel, still holding his drawn pistol. "You all right?"

Noel turned to him with a smile. "I am now. Thanks, Cody. You saved my life."

Cody's blue eyes were alight. "That makes us even now. A man's entitled to have a fair fight. I couldn't let 'em both gang up on you."

Noel nodded. "All right, Leon. On your feet."

Leon hunched on the ground, hiding his face. "No. I can't see."

In exasperation, Noel bent over him. "Stop whining. Some water will flush out the—"

Unexpectedly, there came the barely glimpsed flash of bright steel through the air and the thunk of its impact with something solid. Cody made a strangled noise and staggered into Noel, who caught him just as he sank to his knees.

In shock, Noel gripped him hard, too stunned by the sight of the knife hilt protruding from Cody's chest to think, much less act.

"Cody," he whispered. *"No!"*

Cody's eyes darkened with pain. His gaze shifted, as though seeking Noel's face. A shudder went through his body, and Noel tightened his grip as though to hold his life together by physical strength alone.

"Hang on, kid," he said, his voice raw with grief. "Oh, God."

Cody's eyelids fluttered. "Should have . . . should have checked Raton's boot," he said softly, fading. "A Mex always carries a . . . always in his . . . boot."

He sagged, lifeless in Noel's arms. Stricken, Noel went on holding the dead boy, heedless of Don Emilio and Trask galloping up, heedless of Don Emilio shooting El Raton with two quick, lethal shots, heedless of anything until Trask knelt awkwardly on the ground beside him and took the boy from his grasp.

The old man touched Cody's still face and began to weep. Don Emilio joined him quietly and put his hand on Trask's

SHOWDOWN

shoulder. His hazel eyes, compassionate and filled with sorrow, met Noel's over the old man's bowed head.

There was nothing they could say. Noel pulled himself wearily erect, aware of Cody's blood staining his shirt, and turned on Leon with a swell of rage so strong it blanked every other thought from his mind.

"This is your fault," he said.

Leon, his eyes open again and bloodshot, scrambled back from him, but Noel gripped him by the shirtfront and hauled him to his feet.

"You've gone too far," he said. "From the moment you came into existence you set yourself to create mayhem and anarchy. Now you've done murder—"

"I didn't!" gasped Leon, shrinking from him. "I didn't. El Raton—"

"You set him free," said Noel furiously. "You tampered with his mind. You forced him to kill Cody."

"But Cody was supposed to die!" said Leon. "You know that. He was supposed to—"

With a roar, Noel gripped Leon's throat in his hands and squeezed with all his might. "I . . . don't . . . care!" he said through gritted teeth, seeing nothing through his haze of anger except Leon's terrified face. "This is the last of you!"

Leon clawed at his wrists without effect. His face turned purple, his eyes frantic.

Don Emilio gripped Noel's shoulder. "Fratricide is a bitter crime, amigo. Consider if he is worth it."

Noel could barely hear the man through the roaring in his ears. He didn't care, he thought grimly. He wanted Leon *gone,* forever.

Then the bracelet on his wrist grew painfully hot, breaking through his madness, and the LOC's toneless voice said, "Warning. Time course ending. Prepare for recall. Warning. Time course ending. Prepare for recall."

Startled, Noel forgot what he was doing. His head jerked around and he stared at Don Emilio, who had turned pale and retreated from him.

"Sangre de Cristo," whispered Don Emilio, his eyes widening. "What is this?"

"Good-bye," said Noel, but the darkness of the time stream caught and dissolved him before he could finish the word, and he went hurtling through the void.

EPILOGUE

He materialized with a hard thump onto a wooden floor gouged heavily and full of splinters. His hands were still locked about Leon's throat, and Leon was still jerking at his wrists in an effort to break free.

Around them was a weird darkness and fury, interspersed with flashes of light that illuminated tall masts and crowds of fighting men for brief seconds. The most ungodly din of shouting voices, screams, cannon roars, and clashing swords filled the air, making Noel's head ring.

He smelled blood and gunpowder, tar pitch and fire, and the dank, salty odor of the sea itself. Cannons roared again, making the deck shudder like a living thing.

Flung flat, Noel dropped his grip on Leon, who shouted something incomprehensible and sprang away into the mad crush of fighting men.

A flaming torch swung at Noel, who ducked and lifted his hand to shield his eyes. He was knocked sprawling with the flat side of a cutlass.

A gruff voice boomed, "Stand up and fight, ye sniveling coward! We've a ship to take, aye, and booty to plunder. Get to yer feet and help board that damned merchantman, or I'll have yer guts for my cummerbund!"

He swung the sword at Noel, who scrambled to his feet and ran, knowing in disgust that once again his LOC had failed him and he was no closer to home than before.

ROBERT A. HEINLEIN
THE MODERN MASTER OF SCIENCE FICTION

___TRAMP ROYALE__ 0-441-82184-7/$18.95 (April 1992)__
A never before published first hand account of Robert A. Heinlein's travels around the world. Heinlein takes us on a fascinating and unforgettable journey of our own planet Earth.

__EXPANDED UNIVERSE	0-441-21891-1/$5.50
__FARNHAM'S FREEHOLD	0-441-22834-8/$5.50
__GLORY ROAD	0-441-29401-4/$4.99
__I WILL FEAR NO EVIL	0-441-35917-5/$5.99
__THE MOON IS A HARSH MISTRESS	0-441-53699-9/$4.95
__ORPHANS OF THE SKY	0-441-63913-5/$4.99
__THE PAST THROUGH TOMORROW	0-441-65304-9/$5.95
__PODKAYNE OF MARS	0-441-67402-X/$3.95
__STARSHIP TROOPERS	0-441-78358-9/$4.95
__STRANGER IN A STRANGE LAND	0-441-79034-8/$5.99
__TIME ENOUGH FOR LOVE	0-441-81076-4/$5.99
__THE CAT WHO WALKS THROUGH WALLS	0-441-09499-6/$5.99
__TO SAIL BEYOND THE SUNSET	0-441-74860-0/$5.95

For Visa, MasterCard and American Express orders ($10 minimum) call: 1-800-631-8571

FOR MAIL ORDERS: CHECK BOOK(S). FILL OUT COUPON. SEND TO:

BERKLEY PUBLISHING GROUP
390 Murray Hill Pkwy., Dept. B
East Rutherford, NJ 07073

NAME_____

ADDRESS_____

CITY_____

STATE_____ZIP_____

PLEASE ALLOW 6 WEEKS FOR DELIVERY.
PRICES ARE SUBJECT TO CHANGE WITHOUT NOTICE.

POSTAGE AND HANDLING:
$1.50 for one book, 50¢ for each additional. Do not exceed $4.50.

BOOK TOTAL $ _____

POSTAGE & HANDLING $ _____

APPLICABLE SALES TAX $ _____
(CA, NJ, NY, PA)

TOTAL AMOUNT DUE $ _____

PAYABLE IN US FUNDS.
(No cash orders accepted.)

255

CLASSIC SCIENCE FICTION AND FANTASY

__ **DUNE Frank Herbert 0-441-17266-0/$5.50**
The bestselling novel of an awesome world where gods and adventurers clash, mile-long sandworms rule the desert, and the ancient dream of immortality comes true.

__ **STRANGER IN A STRANGE LAND Robert A. Heinlein**
0-441-79034-8/$5.99
From the *New York Times* bestselling author—the science fiction masterpiece of a man from Mars who teaches humankind the art of grokking, watersharing and love.

__ **THE ONCE AND FUTURE KING T.H. White**
0-441-62740-4/$5.99
The world's greatest fantasy classic! A magical epic of King Arthur in Camelot, romance, wizardry and war. By the author of *The Book of Merlyn*.

__ **THE LEFT HAND OF DARKNESS Ursula K. LeGuin**
0-441-47812-3/$4.99
Winner of the Hugo and Nebula awards for best science fiction novel of the year. "SF masterpiece!"—*Newsweek* "A Jewel of a story."—Frank Herbert

__ **MAN IN A HIGH CASTLE Philip K. Dick 0-441-51809-5/$3.95**
"Philip K. Dick's best novel, a masterfully detailed alternate world peopled by superbly realized characters."
—Harry Harrison

For Visa, MasterCard and American Express orders ($10 minimum) call: 1-800-631-8571

FOR MAIL ORDERS: CHECK BOOK(S). FILL OUT COUPON. SEND TO:

BERKLEY PUBLISHING GROUP
390 Murray Hill Pkwy., Dept. B
East Rutherford, NJ 07073

NAME_____

ADDRESS_____

CITY_____

STATE_____ ZIP_____

PLEASE ALLOW 6 WEEKS FOR DELIVERY.
PRICES ARE SUBJECT TO CHANGE WITHOUT NOTICE.

POSTAGE AND HANDLING:
$1.50 for one book, 50¢ for each additional. Do not exceed $4.50.

BOOK TOTAL	$ ____
POSTAGE & HANDLING	$ ____
APPLICABLE SALES TAX (CA, NJ, NY, PA)	$ ____
TOTAL AMOUNT DUE	$ ____

PAYABLE IN US FUNDS.
(No cash orders accepted.)